JONAH
& FRIENDS
The Short Stories

by
Robert Coulsdon

Front cover: Photo by Robert Coulsdon

© Robert Coulsdon 2023
Published by Robert Coulsdon 2023
First Edition

ISBN: 978-1-7391727-4-9 Paperback
ISBN: 978-1-7391727-5-6 eBook

Printed using paper from sustainable managed forests
by Printed Word Publishing
www.printedwordpublishing.com

For all those people who find themselves
homeless for whatever reason

Acknowledgments

I'd like to thank Wendy, my wife, and Alice Lai, one of my oldest friends, both of whom helped to proof-read and edit the manuscript.

Index

List of Characters i

About Jonah iii

Expectations* 1

Jonah and the High Life 3

Sally the Storekeeper's Wife 12

Mike, Going Down 23

Jonah and the Whale* 34

Spat out in Nineveh 36

It's Tough* 47

Mike, Going Up 48

A Local Hero 58

Chris the Storekeeper 69

Ray's Lad 85

Sarah's Dilemma 96

Walking under a Ladder 111

Jonah's Pink Period 121

Cardboard Christmas* 133

Jonah's Reverie 135

* Poems

Characters

Jonah	'Homeless, lives on the street', buys his 'booze' from Chris' store
Mary	One of the few women in Jonah's society
Mac and Ray	Friends with Jonah
Iain	Reporter for a local newspaper, friend of Andy
Chris	Manager of the small local store where Jonah buys his 'booze'. Married to Sally
Sally	Wife of Chris, the storekeeper
Maurice	Regional Manager for Chris' store
Eileen	Mike's Mother, works in a small shop near the bus station carpark
Mike	Eileen's son
Gill	A corporate events organiser who lives in the flat above Mike
Rogers	Mike's manager
Mrs Serjeant	Rogers' mistress
Andy	Replacement Regional Manager for Chris' store, friend of Iain

Laura	A woman Andy and Chris meet in a bar
Sarah	Friend of Laura
Paul	Young boy who 'befriends' Jonah
Becky	Paul's sister
Ellen	Paul's mother
Kieran	Hair Salon owner
Misha	Assistant in Kieran's Salon

About Jonah

People sometimes ask how Jonah came to wander his way through these stories? The easy answer is he just happens to be there. He's always there, somewhere in the background. Asking for money to buy food. Drinking a can of his favourite strong cider or lager, or maybe a cheap bottle of wine if someone has been particularly generous that day. Or asleep on a bench in a park. And every so often, he bumps into people, usually inadvertently, but sometimes more purposely if he knows they are good for a fag or two, or a small donation.

There's a Jonah in every city or larger town, we've all met him, or avoided him, as he stumbles along the pavement. The clothes may not always be the same, generally shabby, but occasionally bizarre, and he'll usually have a few days stubble, making you wonder why it is that he shaves some days instead of growing a beard? But that's not the type of question Jonah wastes time on, he's a man with a mission, to get enough money for the next drink and, if he's lucky, for a night in a hostel. Shop doorways or cardboard cities are exposed and uncomfortable.

He's learned to be manipulative; he has to be to survive. He gets angry, but that's understandable, given the hardness of his existence compared with the people who pass him by. He's grateful when someone gives him money, afraid of being beaten-up much of the time, and always alone, even when he's with the other street people with whom he hangs out. He has vague memories of a better, earlier life, and sometimes he feels tears welling-up as the images appear and he recalls what he's lost. The problem is that passers-by see only the outstretched hand and shabby clothes, they don't see Jonah. And that's a pity, Jonah deserves to be seen.

So, where did Jonah come from? Nobody seems to know. I found him one lunchtime, as I sat at a pub window. He was wandering along the street opposite, on his way into the city. But where he actually came from is anyone's guess. Apart from other homeless people, I never saw anyone talking to him. People in the homeless hostel might know more but, in a way, it's irrelevant. After all, what does it add to the stories? My interest is the man in the charcoal-coloured overcoat, tied round with string, the one I still imagine walking around the city with an unshaven face and rheumy eyes. The one with the red vinyl shopping bag and the clanking cans of booze

Expectations

Expectations are
Generally unfulfilled,
So, don't expect much.

Jonah and the High Life

The man pushed Jonah away and tried to walk around him as he passed.

"Just a few pence for a cuppa," Jonah persisted, walking alongside him and holding out his hand.

"Piss off". The man looked into Jonah's pale blue, almost grey eyes for a moment and then down at the dirty charcoal coloured coat, tied loosely round the waist with string. "Crawl back to wherever the hell you came from," he growled and pushed past Jonah as he walked away.

"Bloody bastard," Jonah shouted after him.

Jonah didn't mind people refusing him money; generally, they just looked away and tried to escape. What drove him mad were people who insulted him. There was no need to abuse him, just because he needed a little help. The social workers said they could get him new clothes and find him somewhere to live, if he stopped drinking. But booze wasn't a problem to Jonah, he needed it to take away the pain and stress he felt – it made him feel better. And it didn't stop him doing anything because he had nothing else to do.

Upset by the man's reaction, he decided to leave the city and walk to the river to see if he could find any of his mates. There was one place in particular, near a bridge, where they could climb down a few steps, walk along the grassy bank and sit beneath the trees. He could drink most of the morning and then spend the afternoon lying asleep. Besides, Mary might be there and, if she was in a good mood, she might cuddle-up to him as they slept for an hour or two. She was a bit rough maybe, but she was a woman. And there were very few women in Jonah's life.

It was a long walk and the cans felt increasingly heavily in the red vinyl shopping bag he always carried. Jonah imagined sitting in the back of a large limousine with a cocktail cabinet and drinking whisky from a cut crystal glass whilst the chauffeur took him from place to place. Then the women would look at him, "Bloody well fight with each other to get in," he muttered.

He tried to remember, back, to when things might have been different, but it was too long ago, and everything was confused. He had known a woman once, but even then he'd been drinking, and she'd left when she realised he wouldn't stop.

Turning a corner, he saw the bridge ahead and made for the steps leading down to the bank. There was a small group, including Mary, sitting in a circle on the grass. Jonah joined them, lowering himself down and placing his bag beside him.

"Five-pound note, she give me," Mac was saying, "Went up to 'er and thought she was going to refuse at first, but I needed the money. So, I tell 'er I've not eaten for two days. She tries to walk off but when I put me 'and on 'er arm she stops, stares at me, and then gives me the money."

Jonah knew Mac well and often drank with him. "Reckon she fancied yer, do you?" Jonah asked.

Some of the others in the circle laughed.

"Might 'ave," Mac replied defensively.

"More likely she gave you the money 'cos you scared 'er," said Mary. "Young girl on 'er own like that, coming through the passage to the bus station and you pestering 'er. We'll 'ave the bloody police after us again if it gets around, moving us on again. Fucking bastards."

"She's right," said Jonah. "They like to pick on us. Soft bloody target we are."

They sat there silently, considering the matter, and then Mary got up on to her knees and pulled at Jonah's sleeve. "Come on, let's go along the bloody bank."

"She's just after yer bloody booze," Mac shook his head disparagingly.

"And what's wrong with 'im sharing 'is booze if 'e wants?" Mary shouted. "It's none of your fucking business. Anyway, it were only last week you were more than 'appy to let me share yours."

The others laughed and Mac, embarrassed, swore and lay back on the grass, his arms across his eyes, ready to go to sleep.

Jonah got up, grasped his bag and helped Mary to her feet. She gathered together the numerous plastic bags in which she carried her possessions and walked off with him, stumbling occasionally on the uneven ground. They'd rounded a bend in the river when Mary put down her bags and told Jonah to look after them.

"I'm going behind those bushes to 'ave a pee and don't want to 'ear you rustling around, trying to bloody look at me."

"It never crossed me mind, God help me," Jonah shouted. "I don't bloody need to look at an old cow like you."

Booze made Jonah short-tempered. Sometimes he listened to himself shouting without knowing when or why he had started. It was bad enough when his body became uncontrollable but losing control of his mind had begun to scare him more. Sometimes, he would force himself to stop yelling, and shuffle away, but then someone would say something, and the yelling would start again.

Mary ignored him and went behind a bush, chattering away to herself. When she'd finished, she came and lay next to him, resting her head on her arm. Jonah sat against a tree trunk, smoking a roll-up made from dog-ends he'd found in the street.

"Give us a drag," she said, and held out her hand to take it from him.

The cigarette and the heat made Jonah drowsy. He surrendered the stub and shut his eyes. When he woke-up Mary was walking back to the city. He watched as she struggled along the bank, her old purple coat over her arm and her shoulders weighed down by the weight of the plastic bags, bags that bumped rhythmically against her brown trousers with each step she took.

He dozed for a little longer and then got up and started his own way back. Reaching the road, he tried to cadge some money, but a violent refusal pushed him into the path of a young man, who caught him as he stumbled. The man noted the lean face with the golden stubble standing out untidily from the tanned skin and watched the beginnings of panic as Jonah pushed him away. Jonah, suspicious and unsure, watched as the man took the loose change out of his pocket, reached for Jonah's hand and wrapped his fingers around the coins. Without saying anything, the man walked away.

Jonah thanked him profusely to his back, raising his finger to his forehead then bowing slightly at the same time. He clenched the money tightly, there was enough for several cans, and set off for the small grocery store where he bought his booze. The supermarkets in the city centre wouldn't serve him, but Chris, the store manager, wasn't as fussy, he served anybody - so long as they could pay. He acknowledged Chris as he walked in, grunting a greeting, and making his way to the shelf with the extra strong lager. He picked up four cans and took them to the till, counting out his money and placing the coins down on the counter as he did so.

Chris' fingers scrabbled slightly as he picked the coins up. "You ok?" he asked, smiling at Jonah.

Jonah nodded, placed the cans in his bag and left the store making for his favourite bench near the bus station carpark. It was a place he could lie down and sleep after he'd finished drinking; feeling safe as drivers parked their cars or drove away. He walked past the cars, queuing at the entrance, and waved to the woman in the newsagents. She waved back. They were old acquaintances and Jonah cadged cigarettes from her most days, but today he was anxious for a drink. Finally, he reached the seat, sat down and opened a new can of lager.

He enjoyed watching the traffic and, as the day got later, seeing the office workers hurrying home in the rush hour, the hot and dusty streets quietening as the people and cars were replaced by the stillness of empty buildings. The air became cooler and, tired of the continual fight against the soft waves of alcohol, he lay on his side, facing the back of the seat, cradling his bag with his head resting on the arm. He pulled his coat tighter to keep himself warm and fell asleep.

Whilst he slept the traffic became heavier as people returned to the city. Small queues formed as they waited outside restaurants, and the car parks refilled. Jonah became vaguely aware of the confused murmur of people and traffic but dozed until he felt the heat and liquid spreading across his legs and stomach. Placing his hand in

7

his groin, he felt the wetness and swore. it was an irritation to him now, nothing more. Still drowsy, he dozed again, until he felt a sudden pain, a punch thudding heavily into his back.

The next blow made him gasp, his chest tightening and his stomach pushing outwards. He screamed abuse and rolled over, his arms across his body and face to protect them and his knees raised-up, covering his abdomen. Looking through his arms, he saw three youths standing over him and laughing.

"Bastards," Jonah yelled and stood up slowly, feeling the arm of the bench behind him. He tried to move around and put the bench between himself and the youths. "What you want to 'it me for?"

The youths said nothing. The front youth, the one that had hit him, raised his head and stood staring at Jonah with a slight grin, his fist still clenched.

"It'd be different if there wuz only one of you. Wouldn't it, eh?" said Jonah. "Yer wouldn't dare 'it me on yer own, bloody cowards."

One of the other youths moved to his side and Jonah turned instinctively to watch him. He saw the arm with a bottle coming down towards his head too late and only managed to partly parry the blow. He felt a sharp pain and was conscious of nothing else for a brief moment, staggering sideways and clutching at the bench for support. The warm blood trickled slowly down onto his face from the wound and he brushed it away from his eyes.

"Tough old bird, ain't he, Joe?" the first youth turned to the one with the bottle.

The movement distracted Jonah and he was too late to avoid the new blow the first youth struck into his stomach.

He fell to his knees and vomited violently onto his trousers and the ground.

"Not so mouthy now, are you, you fucking old sod?"

Jonah started to panic, looking round for someone to help him, but there was no-one nearby, except for the third youth who'd taken no part in the violence so far. "Can't you stop 'em? I ain't done nothing," Jonah looked into his face, pleading for him to intervene, "I won't tell no-one what happened, only don't let 'em 'it me again."

The youth seemed distressed, but weaker than the other two and Jonah felt a boot pushed solidly in his back. He fell forward, hitting his head against the arm of the bench, and lay there unwilling to risk further punishment.

"Leave him, you've hurt him enough," he heard the third youth say. "You'll fucking kill him if you carry on."

"'E's a bloody disgrace," said the first youth. "Some bloody wino scared Tracy out of 'er mind the other night. Kept pestering 'er for money until she got so scared, she gives 'im five quid. I met 'er at the bus station crying 'er eyes out. Could've been this fucking one, but even if it wasn't, 'e can pass the message on. They ought to be fucking shot, all of 'em."

"Watch out, there's a cop car coming," the second youth pointed down the road. "We need to get out of here fast."

The youths disappeared down a side street and Jonah raised himself slowly to his feet supporting himself on the arm of the bench. Twisting his body he sat down heavily, his back and head aching and blood still dripping onto his face. The car stopped, and he watched apprehensively as two policemen got out and walked over to him.

"Thought I'd seen something," the driver said, and bent forward to look at Jonah. "He's in a bit of a mess, somebody's given him a real beating. Get your torch, it's difficult to see properly, the light is fading."

The second policemen shone a light blindingly into Jonah's eyes.

"Christ, what did you do to deserve this?"

"Bloody bastards. Beat me up. No reason. I was asleep - on the bench." Jonah spoke in short bursts, his head and back still hurting. In his bag there was one last can of lager and, his throat dry, he wanted to take it out and drink it.

"What shall we do with the old boy?" the driver asked. "They won't thank us for taking him down the station and there's no chance of finding out who did this to him."

"God, he stinks," the second policeman said noticing the sharp smell of urine and seeing the vomit on his trousers. "Must have peed himself and been sick when they hit him. I don't fancy having him in the car."

"We can't leave him, the state he's in," the driver was re-examining Jonah's wounds. "Did they hit you anywhere else?"

"Me back," Jonah indicated the spot with his hand. "Me back, they 'it me in me back, the bastards."

"We'll take him down to casualty, they'll soon clean him up and probably keep him in for observation," he heard the driver say. "At least he'll have a comfortable bed for the night."

"Can't we call an ambulance?" the other policeman asked. "God knows what sort of mess he'll make in the car, probably puke up all over the seat."

"It's only a mile. Come-on". The driver took Jonah's arm and began leading him to the car.

"Me bag, want me bag," Jonah pulled away and picked up his red bag before climbing into the back seat. He was unused to the comfort but settled himself down and felt for the last can of lager. He chuckled as he visualised the cocktail cabinet in his imaginary limousine.

"Christ, we'll never get rid of the smell in here," the policeman in the passenger seat was still complaining. "What the hell..."

The can hissed as Jonah pulled the ring and a slight spray hit him in the face as he put it quickly to his mouth and started drinking.

"Let him enjoy it," the driver shook his head. "It'll be the last drink he has for a couple of days, and he's had a hard time. Let's get him to the hospital and then we can sign off. Just don't make a mess," he called to Jonah in the back, "OK?"

Jonah drank more slowly. He played with the lager, holding it in his mouth and then swallowing it. Despite the beating, it hadn't been too bad a day. First a cuddle with Mary and now the back seat of a car, with a drink in his hand, just like one of those business 'gents' with a chauffeur. "It's the bloody high life," he muttered as he finished the can.

Sally, the Storekeeper's Wife

Sally checked her make-up in the mirror, brushed her hair and examined her face critically. She told herself there were lines starting about her eyes and her lips were looking slightly thinner. And her cheeks, one of her best features when she was younger, seemed, to her critical eyes, to lack their previous fullness. She told herself she was tense, that she'd look better once she relaxed. Then, thinking she'd heard a floorboard creak, she looked round nervously in case Chris, her husband, was coming upstairs. She listened intently but there were no more sounds and she decided that Chris must still be busy in the shop below.

She thought back to how she'd planned everything. It had all been so easy, so contemptibly easy, telling Chris she was going for some retail therapy with a friend, that she hadn't bought any clothes for ages and spoiling herself for once would make her feel good.

"Fine, it will be great to have some time to yourself," he'd leant across and kissed her on the cheek. "I know how you hate being stuck in the shop. The girls and I can cope easily for a day." And he'd gone back to his paperwork.

She'd gone shopping on her own, not wanting anyone to see all her purchases and inadvertently tell Chris if he asked how the day had gone. When she returned, she'd shown him the new outfit she'd bought, feeling elegant as she watched herself spin round in front of their long bedroom mirror, but she hadn't shown him the expensive lingerie she'd chosen. She'd hidden that in the bottom of her wardrobe, so Chris wouldn't see it. Today, wearing it for the first time, it felt silky and sensual and she smiled to herself as she imagined the effect it would have when she and Maurice began to make love. How it would arouse him as she undressed, and he saw her step out of it.

Chris would never be like Maurice. She hated the way he fussed around her. It was irritating and demeaned him, his puppy-like anxiety to make her feel happy and ingratiate himself. And it wasn't just her, he was like it with the customers and the girls in the store. Maurice was different, worldly and strong. She reached for her perfume and sprayed generous bursts on her neck and wrists. If Chris hadn't been so blind, he would have realised from the beginning that Maurice wanted her, and she told herself the affair mightn't have started if he'd been more assertive and successful, and she'd respected him more.

As the area manager, Maurice was required to visit the store regularly, but his visits had become more frequent since Chris had introduced them. Maurice was everything Chris wasn't, tall, confident and a powerful man in the company. She'd known immediately that he fancied her, and flattered by his obvious desire, and led on by her own attraction to him, she'd tried to use him - to achieve her ambitions for Chris to move to a bigger store, to become more successful. Maurice listened and encouraged her, giving her a hug after they'd met a few times and then a welcoming kiss on the cheek a couple of visits later. And then, one morning, whilst she was making him a coffee, he pushed her hair aside and kissed the back of her neck.

She recalled her reaction, the speed with which she had turned and kissed him back. She 'd kissed him because he offered her the opportunity of something better than the small flat above the store, the flat with its cheap fittings and boxes piled high on the stairway. And she'd kissed him because she wanted to join the rest of the world that carried on its frantic, exciting life, despite never featuring in Chris's meticulously crafted reports.

"Tell Chris you're going shopping, or out with a friend and let's spend a day together," Maurice had put his arms around her, pressing himself against her. And she had agreed, afraid of being discovered, but unwilling to risk upsetting him and giving up on her dreams.

The store opened early and closed late. It was convenient for the locals and sold groceries, vegetables and household items. It also sold beer and spirits and was used by the local winos because Chris didn't mind who he served. But Sally loathed the winos, they were unpredictable and smelt of urine. She grimaced as she remembered Jonah, one of Chris's regulars, being thrown out of a supermarket in the city centre, cursing and waving his fist in the air. And then she'd watched with horrified fascination as he'd taken his revenge by peeing in an unsteady line that dribbled down one of the large front windows.

Today, though, would be different, enabling her to get away from the drabness that immersed her. She examined her face for the last time; it would do. Satisfied, she grabbed her handbag from the bed and checked herself again in the long mirror. Her face might be showing signs of ageing, but she still had a good figure. Her stomach was tight, and her close-fitting trousers showed off her slim hips. When she got downstairs, Chris had just finished serving at the checkout. She kissed him cursorily and said she'd be back late afternoon. Then she hurried out of the store hearing him calling 'enjoy yourself' as she left.

Maurice had arranged to meet her several streets away, but, at first, she couldn't see him. Then she heard her name and saw him waving out of a car window. It wasn't the car he normally drove; it was older and dirtier, and she wondered why he'd changed it. He opened the passenger door and, when she'd got in, she asked about the car. He said his usual car was in a garage waiting for repairs, but she picked-up a hesitation in his voice that suggested another reason he didn't want to disclose. As they drove to the hotel he'd chosen, she found herself feeling unexpectedly tense and kept up a friendly but meaningless chatter. He'd said it was 'a nice little hotel' on the outskirts of a town some twenty miles away, but it was part of a national chain of budget hotels, in a run-down area near to the local railway station. She followed him into reception, embarrassed by the obvious purpose of their visit and waited whilst Maurice signed the register. He took the key and smiled as he led her to the room.

The room was utilitarian, with a large double bed, cheap fitted furniture and a slightly soiled carpet. It had none of the softness and luxury she'd imagined, none of the polished refinement. And neither did Maurice; as soon as he'd closed the door, he took her handbag from her shoulder and placed it on a chair, put his arms around her and kissed her hungrily. Sally pulled away, trying to come to terms with the unexpectedly austere surroundings and his impatience. She'd expected something more romantic and practised from him.

"We've got time, slow down, we don't have to rush." She placed her hands against his chest, gently, but firmly pushing him away. "And it's too light in here, people might see us, we're on the ground floor." She turned and walked round the bed to close the curtains.

He followed and, as soon as the curtains were closed, took hold of her shoulders, turning her round to face him. "I want you now," he kissed her again, trying to usher her towards the bed, "I've been waiting for this for weeks."

"My shoes," she said, resisting his pressure, "I've still got my shoes on."

"Kick them off." He smiled down and, moving away, pulled off his tie, folded it and placed it with his jacket on the chair on which he'd put her bag. Then he sat down, unlaced his shoes and placed them together neatly on the floor.

She took off her shoes as he'd told her to but stayed standing by the foot of the bed. Unhappy with the rapidity of everything that was happening she wanted to slow things down but felt frozen, unable to exercise any control. He rejoined her, pulled back the duvet and then manoeuvred her backwards, one hand holding her against him, the other reaching under her jumper, fingers trying awkwardly to undo the catch of her bra. She stood still, upset by his clumsiness and the lack of care he was showing, and then pushed his hand away.

"Here, let me do it." She reached behind her back, and undid the catch, and then held her arms up with a feeling of resigned acceptance. He pulled her jumper over her head and dropped it, together with her new, unnoticed bra, on the floor. As he did so, she thought about Chris - vaguely at first, but with an increasing sense of guilt as she visualised him. Kind, slightly plump and anxious Chris, working back in the store, unaware of what she was doing. She smiled briefly at the vision. Then she felt Maurice's nail catching her as he slid his hand under her trousers and attempted to stimulate her.

"That's right, enjoy it," he said misreading the shudder and the small cry she let out. "Feels good for me as well."

He attempted to slide her trousers off. But, instead of moving her hips and helping him, she stayed still and touched his face to get his attention. "You will help Chris to get a better shop, won't you, Maurice?" She was upset, humiliated by the way she was being used, but, at the same time, clinging on to her dream of Chris being promoted and being able to move from the small, untidy flat in which they were living.

"Of course, I've said I will." His answer was immediate but lacked sincerity. "Let's talk about it later. But first, let's enjoy ourselves whilst we have the opportunity."

"It would mean a lot to me as well as Chris," she persisted, "I can't stand the thought of staying in that wretched shop and pokey flat for ever. You do care about how I feel, don't you?"

"Sshh," he put his finger against his own lips in a sign she should stop talking, "You have my word." He stood looking down at her, making her feel embarrassed. Then he kissed her again and eased her trousers and panties over her hips, leaving her standing there naked, whilst he remained dressed. Anxious to get things over, she began to undo his shirt buttons and then pushed down his trousers and underpants.

"That's better," he stepped out of his trousers and underwear and reached down, sliding his hand across her stomach, before placing his finger inside her again and trying to arouse her. "I knew we'd be good together." He moved her backwards, until she felt the bed against the back of her knees and fell onto it. Smiling, he hovered over her, and then lowered his body onto hers. Almost immediately, he began to thrust into her groin, but couldn't enter her. Resigned to what was happening, she helped him and gasped as he forced himself inside. He misread her reaction again and began pushing, not waiting for her. He came quickly, gasping loudly as he did and, when he'd finished, rolled off and lay by her side.

Sally lay still, feeling tearful, knowing she'd been used and meant nothing to the man.

"Pity you couldn't come as well. Maybe later. Do you mind me having a cigarette? I always like a smoke afterwards."

"It's not allowed," she lay still, sore and sweaty from his body, "Hotel rules." She pointed at a notice on the wall opposite.

"I'll open the window and hold the cigarette outside," he pulled his jacket off the chair and took out the old-fashioned brass lighter he always carried. "My grandfather's, this was, but it still works every time." He spun the wheel against the flint to demonstrate. "There, what did I tell you? Lights like a dream." He caressed the lighter, holding it in front of him and examining it with affection.

"I'm going to take a shower," she raised herself off the bed.

" Can't it wait?" he sounded irritable. "Give me half an hour or so and we can do it again."

"I'm too sore," She sat up and swung her feet over the side of the bed, noting he still had his socks on.

He watched as she walked across to the shower, then turned and opened the window for his smoke, not noticing how she was biting her lip to restrain the angry tearfulness she felt. Concern for Chris's career had been her excuse, the justification that over-rode her feelings of guilt. The truth was that she had set out to seduce Maurice, knowing he wanted her. And she was bored with Chris, kind, considerate Chris who waited for her, trying to time his own orgasms with the ones she generally faked.

Maurice had finished his cigarette and closed the window when she returned, and tried to get her back onto the bed again. This time she resisted, steeling herself when he touched her and humouring him into leaving. They had a drink in the bar and then drove back without talking. He played the car radio loudly and tapped the steering wheel in time with the music.

She found his pleasure obnoxious. Her face burned and she became increasingly nervous as they got nearer the store. Distressed and dissatisfied, and no longer believing Maurice would help promote Chris as he'd promised, she began to be scared they might be seen. And, at the same time, she felt humiliated, both by the way in which she'd been treated and by her own naivety in trusting the man.

"Drop me at the end of this street, please. I'll walk the rest of the way." She placed her hand on the door catch, in anticipation of getting out.

"Can't let you walk," he looked quickly at her, smiled and squeezed her leg, "Not after this afternoon."

"Please let me out before we get too close to the store." His grotesque misinterpretation of her mood appalled her. "If we get any closer, somebody might see us."

"Nobody will see us. And, if they do, you can always say we met whilst you were shopping." He began to run his free hand up the inside of her thigh.

"Look, you've got to stop at the lights. I'll get out here." She grabbed the door handle. "Whatever you do, please don't say anything to anybody, Chris must never find out what happened today."

It was a hopeless request. She knew, before she finished speaking, that she would be included in his latest list of conquests when he stood in the next bar, drinking with his friends.

"Don't worry, it's our secret," he said and leaned across to kiss her as she started to get out.

Sally hurried away without looking back and kept her eyes down as he drove past. She checked her appearance in the 'ladies' in one of the large stores, searching for give-away marks and panicking as she noticed a slight rash that his bristles had caused on her cheek. Repairing the damage with her make-up, she rehearsed her story and examined it for loopholes. Satisfied, she bought a jumper she'd seen previously and began her walk home.

As she approached the store she saw Jonah, his lean figure wrapped in the old charcoal-coloured overcoat he always wore. He started to cross the street, not looking for traffic; intent only on buying the super strength lager he drank. A car came round the corner and braked hard to avoid him, stopping with its bumper almost touching his legs. Sally recognised the car; it was the one she'd been sitting in just a short time before. She wondered what Maurice was doing there: concerned Chris would see him.

Jonah appeared startled and then became angry, yelling at the driver through the windscreen. She saw Maurice's arm raised and his hand violently motioning Jonah out of the way. He was shouting at Jonah, his face contorted in fury. And, in response, Jonah started banging his fist on the bonnet and shouting back. He seemed pleased with the banging and pounded harder as Maurice became more agitated. For the first time in her life, Sally found herself on Jonah's side.

The driver's door opened, and Maurice began to climb out. Then, seemingly, he changed his mind and, shutting the door again, revved-up the engine. Jonah stopped banging when the engine noise changed and hurried to the safety of the pavement. The car moved away and Sally glimpsed Maurice's wife looking straight ahead as the car passed, tense and unhappy.

The danger past, Jonah shouted and stuck two fingers up. The car braked hard and started to pull back into the kerb. Jonah scuttled into the store and the car pulled away again, nearly colliding with a van. Sally heard renewed shouting behind her and, enjoying Maurice's discomfort, followed Jonah into the shop.

"Seen that fucking bastard before," Jonah was saying to Chris. "Been in here sometimes."

"It was Maurice, the area manager," Sally said as she kissed Chris 'hello', trying to behave as normally as possible. "He nearly ran Jonah over. Everything ok?"

"Yes. Enjoy your shopping? What did you get?"

"Oh, just a jumper. But I enjoyed wandering around and trying things on. I'll show you the jumper when you come upstairs." She walked out through the back of the store and climbed the staircase up to the flat.

Chris served Jonah and, when he'd gone, went up to see Sally, his face was pink, and she could see he was excited.

"I heard some really surprising news whilst you were out," he didn't pause to let her speak, "and it may mean we can get a better store."

"That's wonderful," Sally was surprised, she hadn't believed that Maurice really intended to help them - and certainly not so quickly. "Is that why Maurice was here?"

"Oh, Maurice hasn't been in here. That's the news", Chris said. "He's not the area manager anymore. He and the manager over at Berwick Street were working some kind of a scam. They've taken thousands of pounds over the past few years. Anyway, the auditors found out and they were both fired yesterday. Andy, a guy I know, has been appointed area manager in Maurice's place. We've always got on ok and I was never going to get anywhere whilst Maurice was in charge, but with Andy taking over I thought I'd apply for the 'Berwick Street' job. It's a much better store than this one and it may be the chance we've been looking for."

Mike, Going Down

Mike glanced at his watch as he waited whilst a lorry manoeuvred into a narrow entrance. He checked his hair in the car mirror. The girl at the salon hadn't done a bad job, the blond highlights looked good, particularly with his dark suit, and the hair lay straight and neat against his shirt collar.

"Every inch the successful young salesman," he murmured to himself, "The boss can't fail to be impressed." But, at the same time, in the back of his mind, he felt anxious about the reason for being called into the office so late on a Friday afternoon.

The traffic started to move again, and Mike slipped the car into gear. The car was a real bonus, replacing the old banger he'd driven before he'd got the job some months previously. He turned right towards the car park and past the small newsagents where his mother worked. The car park, thank God, wasn't full; he glanced at his watch again, concerned about the time, and pulled into one of the empty spaces. Grabbing his case and his jacket from the back seat, he locked the door and walked across to say a brief 'hello' to his mother. She was standing outside the shop waving a finger at a local homeless guy, who stood in front of her grinning like a naughty schoolboy. When she looked-up and saw Mike she smiled before returning to admonishing the man.

"Here, now be off with you, Jonah," his mother pulled a packet of cigarettes from her pocket, took two out and gave them to the ragged figure. Jonah was a familiar sight in the town, struggling along in his charcoal-coloured overcoat, drawn tight with coarse string, and carrying a red vinyl shopping bag wherever he went. "And don't look up at me with those sad old eyes trying to cadge some more," his mother said, "There aren't any more today."

"You're a good woman," Jonah touched his forehead with his finger and turned and noticed Mike. "'Ave you got a light, mister?"

"Sorry, I don't smoke. Here," Mike passed some money to his mother, "Give him some matches from me, please."

"And can you spare some change for a cup of coffee," Jonah eyed the money in Mike's hand, "I 'aven't 'ad a drink all day."

Mike's mother snorted in disbelief when she came back out of the shop and heard what Jonah was saying. "If you believe that, you'll believe anything." She turned to Jonah and gave him the packet of matches. "That's my son you're talking to. You've had cigarettes from me and matches from him. Now be off with you and go and bother someone else."

"A few pence ain't going to bother a successful young gent, like him." Jonah looked Mike in the eyes and grinned again.

"How can you resist him?" Mike guessed it was a practised grin, but still gave Jonah a few coins.

"Quite easily when he comes round asking for cigarettes almost every day. Go on Jonah, be off," his mother pointed along the street, "I'd like to have a chat with my son now."

Jonah lit one of the cigarettes and inhaled deeply, then nodded, picked up his red bag and started off along the street.

"Poor chap, it's dreadful to end up like that. I often wonder what happened to make him like he is," she shook her head, "Anyway, what brings you into town so late on a Friday? You normally rush home to start the weekend early."

"Oh, I got a call from the manager, he wants to see me about something."

"Well, you certainly look smart," his mother reached up and flicked a piece of fluff off his shoulder, "And I'm getting used to the hair, although I'll never understand what was wrong with the colour you were born with."

"You've got to move with the times, Mum," he gave her a quick kiss on the cheek, "I'd better get going or I'll be late. My meeting's scheduled for five-thirty and I've got a few things to sort out beforehand."

"Well, if I'm still here when you get out, pop your head round the door on your way back to the car park and let me know how your meeting went," his mother said. "And, if I've closed up the shop, ring me this evening."

The office was almost deserted when Mike walked in. He looked at some papers, which had been left on his desk, dealt with a few e-mails, and knocked on the manager's door.

"Ah, Mike, sit down," the manager indicated a seat at a small table he used for meetings, reached into his desk drawer and pulled out an envelope. "I'm sorry to ask you to come in so late on a Friday afternoon," he got up, walked across and sat down opposite Mike at the table.

"No problem," Mike smiled, wondering what was in the envelope. "What did you want to see me about?"

The manager paused before talking. "There's no easy way of saying this," he shook his head before continuing, "I'm sorry but things are not working out as well as we'd hoped and we're going to have to let you go."

Mike was confused and felt a sudden panic as he took in what the other man was saying. "I'm sorry, I don't understand," he heard himself talking quickly, took a conscious breath and slowed himself down. "My figures are ok, I'm on target, so what aren't you happy with?"

"It's not your figures that are the issue," the manager hesitated momentarily before deciding how to continue, "It's the way you interact with your colleagues – some of them have mentioned problems with your attitude and it's affecting the team's morale. I realise this may be a shock for you and you've only been here for a few months, but it's been decided that it's better if we terminate your contract now, rather than push the decision down the road until later."

"But this is the first anyone's mentioned any issues to me. I'd really like to sit down with you, or the persons concerned, to see if we can talk things through, resolve whatever's upsetting them."

"I'm sorry," the other man said, "but the decision's already been made."

"But surely, we can sit down and review what's gone wrong?" Mike felt devastated by what he was hearing. "I know there have been issues when I've been sorting out customers' problems, particularly where the support team don't understand a customer's point of view." Mike thought back to the occasions on which differences of opinions had caused arguments and recognised the person the manager was referring to. He wondered whether it was wise to mention her by name, but decided he had nothing to lose if he did. "I know I've had a couple of run-ins with Mrs Serjeant, but she's the only person I'm aware of upsetting, in which case this all seems very unfair."

"I'm sorry, I can't discuss your relationship with individual members of staff, that wouldn't be fair to them. But there have been suggestions that you're too ready to blame the sales support for issues raised by the customers." The manager paused, then passed the envelope he'd been holding across to Mike. "We do realise this may come as a bit of a shock, although you must have been aware of some of the tension surrounding you, so, as you'll see from our letter, we're prepared to be generous and we're giving you an extra month's notice whilst you look for a new position. And, obviously, we'll give you a reference based on your sales performance. Other than that, there's nothing more I can say, except to wish you all the best and hope you've found the past few months here useful."

"What about my car and working out my notice?" Mike asked.

"We've already looked at re-defining the sales areas, and we'd like you to introduce members of the existing salesforce to your contacts over the next two weeks, but after that you're on gardening leave. Obviously, you can keep the car until that ends. As I said earlier, we're sorry it's got to be this way, but you're young and I'm confident you'll be able to find a new position and make a success of your career."

"So, is that it?" Mike shook his head in disbelief.

"As I said, I'm afraid the decision has been made."

The manager stood up and held out his hand, but Mike shook his head, ignoring the other man's gesture, collected his personal effects from his desk and slammed the outer office door angrily behind him as he left. He looked for his mother as he approached the car park, but the shop was shut, so he hurried to his car.

On Friday evenings he normally ate at his flat and then met friends for a drink. Tonight, he needed a drink immediately and drove to a quiet pub just outside the town centre. He threw his jacket into the back of the car, pulled his tie down and unbuttoned his collar. The pub was empty when he walked in, and he sat on one of the high stools by the bar. The first pint went down quickly, and he ordered another. His feelings of insecurity were gnawing at him. He had just four months to find a job and, if he didn't, he wondered how long he would be able to keep paying the rent on his flat. The car would go too, and suddenly the street seemed very close. He knew his mother would be happy for him to move back home, but the idea appalled him.

"Christ, I'm pissed-off with being pushed around," he told himself. "Half my life is spent being nice to difficult people and then they throw me out of work." He brought his glass down hard on the counter, surprising himself with the force.

The barman looked up.

"Sorry." Mike smiled at him, anxious not to cause any trouble, but the angry thoughts kept on coming. "Calming angry customers because some fool in the office has upset them and then calming the fool in the office because they think I've taken the customer's side. Bugger the car, I'll catch a bus." He drained his glass and ordered another pint, but this time he drank it more slowly.

"Are you all done now?" The barman picked up his glass when Mike finished drinking.

"Yes, thanks," Mike got off the stool and was surprised as he staggered back slightly. "Better get something to eat," he muttered and decided to buy some bread at a small supermarket he'd seen, just down the road from the pub and then order a curry later when he got home. The cool evening air made him feel better and, by the time he reached the supermarket, he decided he was sober enough to drive. As he approached the supermarket, the automatic door opened, and Jonah pushed past him.

"Out me bloody way," Jonah muttered, not raising his head to see who he had bumped into.

"Hey take it easy." Mike tried to catch Jonah's attention, expecting him to remember their earlier meeting. "It's me, we met this afternoon. My mum gave you some cigarettes."

Jonah weaved his way down the street without replying, the lager cans clanking against each other in the red bag. Mike watched as he went and then entered the shop. He looked for the bread and saw a man filling some refrigerated cabinets at the far end of the store. "I see you know Jonah," Mike nodded towards the shop door.

The man looked across, smiled, and carried on stacking the cabinet. "Yes, he calls in from time to time. A lot of places won't serve him, but he's harmless enough and he generally comes in later, when the store's not busy. Quite a character, isn't he?"

"Yeah, bums cigarettes off my mother," Mike nodded, "Have you got any bread?"

"Over there, in the next aisle," the man pointed in the direction of the bakery section. "There's not much left, I'm afraid."

As he walked past, Mike knocked against the trolley of refrigerated goods the man was using to refill the shelves. He apologised and the man caught the smell of alcohol on his breath. Young guys who'd been drinking worried him, it made them unpredictable. He'd sent the staff home earlier, as the store hadn't been busy that evening, and there was only him and his wife serving. He felt apprehensive, undecided whether to humour the other man or hurry him out.

Mike reached the bakery section and picked up one of the loaves that had been baked on the premises. The loaf was unwrapped, and he squeezed it, to make sure it was still fresh. But, as he squeezed, he fumbled the loaf and it fell on the floor, despite his juggling efforts to catch it. He noticed some more bread on a lower shelf and, deciding it looked tastier, reached up to place the dropped loaf back where he'd found it.

"I think you'd better take that loaf; you can't put it back." The storeman had followed him from the other aisle and Mike, surprised by hearing his voice immediately behind him, spun round. He was still holding the loaf, his arm raised to place it back on the shelf, and his elbow caught the other man across the face. The man yelled and staggered backwards, dropping down onto his knees, his hands clutching his nose.

"You bastard," the storeman took his hands away from his face and saw the blood that was running from his nose. "What the hell did you do that for?" He got up slowly, watching Mike as he did so.

Mike was shocked and tried to take hold of the man's arm and help him. "I'm sorry, it was an accident," he tried to explain, "I didn't mean to hit you, you just surprised me, I hadn't realised you were there."

"Take your hands off me," the man shrugged him away and Mike let go as he'd been asked, appalled by what had happened. "You bloody assaulted me. Sally, Sally" he shouted to his wife who was in another part of the store, "Call the police, this guy's just hit me."

A woman appeared at the other end of the aisle and threw up her hands when she saw her husband's face, then hurried towards him. "What have you done?" She glared at Mike, and he tried to explain it had been an accident, that he'd been surprised and elbowed her husband by mistake when he'd swung round. But the woman ignored what he was saying. "Look this way Chris," she turned her husband's face towards her, intent on trying to wipe the blood away from his nose with a tissue. She kept glancing across whilst she wiped and, seeing the consternation on Mike's face, became braver, realising he wasn't going to hit out again.

"They could send you down for this." She was angry now, "Try explaining that to your family. You could lose your job, lose everything for this."

"It was an accident," Mike shouted back at her "I didn't mean to hit him." He took out his wallet thrust a note at the woman for the loaf and left the shop, running back to his car, wanting to get home, to get back to the security of his flat. He felt angry as he drove. Angry with the shopkeeper for surprising him. Angry with the company for sacking him. And angry at the world which seemed to be moving so quickly to exclude him.

He parked the car and walked the remaining few yards to his flat. Inside, he still felt tense, took a beer from the fridge and turned the TV on, but was too distracted to watch. The fear of detection and his uncertain future were scaring him, and he no longer felt like eating. He just wanted to drink, to find a temporary oblivion.

He took another beer from the fridge and returned to the lounge as the news came on. 'A shopkeeper was beaten up and robbed today...'

He realised it couldn't be about the shopkeeper he'd just elbowed but swore and turned the TV off. As he did so, the telephone rang.

"It's mum", her voice sounded hesitant. "I've been trying to get you for ages. How did your meeting go?"

"Rotten, I'll call you back in the morning," he replied.

"Why? What happened? I thought you were doing so well."

"So did I mum, but somebody decided my face didn't fit and I've got four months to find another job." Her questions made him feel trapped and he swallowed another mouthful of beer. "Look, I'll call you in the morning. I don't want to talk about it now."

He said 'goodbye' and put the receiver down, shivering involuntarily as he thought about the news report and the similar report that might be broadcast on the local news the following morning. He opened another can, drank the beer and decided to go to bed. But he couldn't sleep. He turned repeatedly beneath the duvet, his jaws clenched so tightly they began to ache.

"How could you be so stupid?" His mental debate continued without his conscious intervention. "You should have stayed and explained to the police that you didn't mean to hit him." The suddenness with which everything had happened still bewildered him. He kept telling himself that without the beers he wouldn't have swung round as violently as he did, and the man wouldn't have been hurt.

He moaned, wishing he could go to sleep and forget. One bloody accident and you could end up paying for ever. It was all the bloody company's fault, and he cursed the manager for his dismissal and Mrs Serjeant for being so bloody vindictive.

As he replayed the incident, mentally trying to get it into perspective, he kept returning with horrible fascination to meeting Jonah in the doorway. He'd told the storekeeper he knew Jonah and that Jonah bummed cigarettes from his mother. Again and again, the small bent figure in a charcoal-coloured overcoat shuffled across his nightmare vision.

"Hey, take it easy. It's me, we met this afternoon." The words haunted him, and he wished he'd never said them. "Did you recognise me?" he asked repeatedly.

He couldn't catch the reply. The ragged figure pushed him aside, muttering as it weaved its way through his imagination. He lay there, unable to dismiss it from his mind as it stumbled down the street. It carried its secret with it; the cans in the red vinyl shopping bag clanking against each other with each step it took.

Jonah and the Whale

His God said unto Jonah that
Great wickedness he saw,
And bade him go to Nineveh
And tell them sin no more.

But Jonah didn't want to go
And went down to the sea
He found a ship to Tarshish
And did his best to flee.

Then God sent down a great wind,
An almighty tempest blew,
And lots were cast to find out
Who'd brought evil on the crew.

And when they heard that Jonah
Had fled before the Lord,
They cried to God, picked Jonah up,
And threw him overboard.

A whale then swallowed Jonah
And to a great depth dived,
For three days Jonah lay inside
Amazed that he'd survived.

There, hidden from the sight of God,
He found his faith restored,
And made a vow from thenceforth
To carry out God's word.

So, God then caused the great fish
To vomit Jonah out,
He landed back on dry land
And turned himself about.

The next day Jonah rose up
To Nineveh he went
And preached it would be overthrown
'Unless people repent'.

The people heard his message
Of death in forty days,
Wore sackcloth and then promised to
Give up their evil ways.

Spat out in Nineveh

Jonah struggled along the road into town, his charcoal-coloured overcoat pulled tightly round him with string and his old red shopping bag weighed down with some cans of super strength lager and the few possessions he had left. He muttered as he went, ignoring the people around him for once and chattering to himself about why the whale had spat out the biblical Jonah.

"You're a Jonah," Mac had said, "Things always go wrong when you're about."

And Jonah he had stayed. Nobody called him by his real name anymore, even Jonah no longer thought of himself by it. But Mac's accusation bothered him. "Bloody fish spat 'im out after three days. Must 'ave been a bloody reason, otherwise 'e'd 'ave died in its bloody belly," he muttered.

He crossed the road, entered the shopping precinct and made for the fountain, hoping to see Ray or Mac, or one of the other guys there. As it happened, he was in luck, and could see Mac and Ray sitting on the wall that contained the water. The pond hadn't been cleared out as it usually had and there were a couple of plastic drink bottles and some litter floating in it. Mac staggered to his feet as Jonah approached and raised his arms, lager can in his hand, as he made a cross to ward Jonah off. Ray pulled him back down and they sat leaning against each other, laughing.

"Bastards," Jonah sat down with them, took a can from his bag and pulled the ring. The can hissed and the lager frothed out. He put it to his lips and drank, anxious not to lose any. "Got any fags?" He looked across at his two mates.

"Cost yer'," Mac said and Ray nodded.

"Bloody get me own," said Jonah and stood up unsteadily. "Spare some coppers for a cuppa?" He asked each person as they walked by, holding out his hand as he spoke. But nobody gave him any money and eventually he gave up and sat back down again muttering "Bastards" under his breath.

"Gotta 'ave a pee," Mac got up and walked towards an alley which led to the service road behind the shops.

"Bloody disgrace," said Jonah, "No bloody loos anywhere. Keep shuttin' 'em. Where the 'ell do they expect us to pee?"

He got up and asked passing shoppers for money again but, as he accosted them, the shoppers looked away and avoided his outstretched hand. Frustrated by his failure to cadge money for fags, Jonah looked around for another possible source of a smoke. A short distance away some boys were sitting on a bench, drinking cans of coke. One of them lit a cigarette, sharing it with his friend next to him. Jonah made his way towards them. "Got a spare fag?" he asked. "'Aven't 'ad a smoke all day."

"Get your own fucking cigarettes," the boy said, shaking his head.

The boy next to him finished his can and threw it down. "Did you see the football on telly last night?" He didn't wait for an answer. Instead, he got up, dribbled the can a couple of yards and then turned and kicked it towards the others. "What a goal!"

Two of the other lads jumped up and the three of them began kicking the can. One of them miskicked and the can shot between the other two, landing in front of Mac as he shambled back towards the fountain.

"Take yer on," Mac challenged them. He knocked the can from one unsteady foot to the other.

"Beat you bloody winos any day," said the boy who'd started the game. He tackled Mac and passed it to one of his friends who backed into a woman as he tried to control it.

"Come on you lot, break it up." A security guard trapped the can under his foot and picked it up. "You're spoiling it for everyone. If you want to play games, go somewhere else." He waited whilst the boys gathered their things together and watched them go before turning round and going back to his usual spot.

When he'd moved off, Jonah saw one of the boys look round to make sure the guard had gone, nudge one of his mates and say something. The boys stopped walking, and one reached into his bag, took out a plastic bottle, and ran back to the fountain. He emptied the contents into the water, throwing the bottle in afterwards. Then, stopping to make a V-sign in the direction of the security guard, he ran back to his mates laughing. Foam began forming in the fountain and overflowing the concrete wall. Shoppers started pointing and calling out to one another, alerting the guard who called for assistance.

Two other security guards arrived, bringing plastic fencing to place around the pool and stop people slipping on the soapy water. As they began erecting the fence one of them turned to Jonah and his companions and waved them away, telling them to leave the precinct and go somewhere they couldn't interfere with the shoppers.

"Told yer there's always trouble when 'e's around," Mac said to Ray as he gathered his coat and cans together. "Jonah by bloody name and Jonah by fucking nature."

"Just move on," the guard was sounding impatient.

"We're goin'," said Mac. "It ain't bloody 'ealthy staying around 'im." And he and Ray staggered off, arms around each other as they disappeared into the crowd, leaving Jonah on his own.

Jonah was aching for a smoke, but he still didn't have any money. He decided to cadge some cigarettes from Eileen in the small store she worked in, outside the city centre. It was about ten minutes away, opposite a small jeweller's, a family business with panelled walls and glass fronted cabinets. Jonah had peered through the door one day but been ushered away by one of the assistants.

"Mornin'. And 'ow are yer?" Jonah said as he approached Eileen's till. She was a large woman, in her early fifties, with short blond hair.

"Fine. How about you?" she replied.

"Not too bad. Mind yer, I'd be a lot better if I'd 'ad a smoke. Can't spare a few fags, could yer?"

Eileen reached under the counter, took out a packet she kept especially for Jonah and gave him a couple of the remaining cigarettes. "Do you know, I think you only come and talk to me when you're out of cigarettes." She waved her finger at him. "Anyway, smoking's bad for you, you should give it up."

"Ah've tried to cut down," Jonah said, "For pity's sake, ah 'aven't 'ad a smoke all day."

"And another thing," it was all part of a regular game they played, "When are you going to give up drinking?"

"Ah'm trying to take it in moderation," he grinned, looking at her out of the corner of his eye as he took the cigarettes, "But it's difficult to give up fags at the same time."

He searched in his pockets and then in his red vinyl bag for some matches. Eileen took a box from the rack and handed it to him.

"And don't light up in here," she told him, "Wait 'til you get outside."

Jonah put one cigarette in his mouth and the others in his pocket. He muttered 'thanks' and raised the hand carrying the matchbox in a goodbye gesture as he shuffled out of the store.

As soon as he was outside Jonah lit the cigarette and inhaled deeply. There was a bench on the opposite side of the road, just along from the jewellers, and he sat down on it, pulling another can from his red vinyl bag. As he smoked and drank, he could see Eileen stacking some shelves near the tobacconist's doorway.

A large grey car pulled up a few yards away and three men got out. Two of them walked towards the jewellers, the third staying by the car, watching the shop door. The driver kept the car's engine running.

Jonah spotted an opportunity to beg some money, got up and walked towards the man by the car. "'Ave yer got a few pence for a cuppa?" Jonah stood in front of the man with his hand extended.

The man motioned Jonah away.

"Just a few pence," Jonah stood his ground. "Only ah 'aven't 'ad an 'ot drink all day."

"Piss off," the man pushed Jonah aside with his arm.

"Don't you bloody tell me to 'piss off'," Jonah recovered his balance and confronted the man, annoyed by the brush-off. "Ah've got as much bloody right to this bloody pavement as you 'ave."

"For Christ's sake piss off, you stupid old sod." The man was agitated and pushed Jonah aside violently.

Jonah stumbled and nearly fell. He stopped himself by catching hold of a signpost.

"Hey, you leave him alone," Eileen had seen what happened and rushed out from her shop. She shouted across the street, enraged at the way the man had pushed Jonah.

Jonah started shouting, but now he was scared of the man and kept his distance. He waved his fist theatrically as Eileen crossed the road.

"Pick on someone who can stand up for himself," Eileen shouted. But the man had turned away from her. "I'm talking to you," she tapped his shoulder and was suddenly afraid as he turned to face her.

Until then she'd acted unthinkingly. Jonah was defenceless, a gabby old man with nothing to back up the stream of insults he was shouting. The man stared at her, deciding what to do, and she backed away. Jonah had stopped shouting. As she watched the man's face, he smiled, reached into his pocket and pulled out a handful of change.

"Here, give this to the old man," he placed it in her hand hurriedly, "And sorry if I hurt him." He turned back to watch the shop door.

"You can't go round assaulting people and then giving them a couple of pounds to forget it," Eileen was confused and stared at the money.

"Look, it's the best I can do," the man continued watching the door. "It's what he wanted in the first place, for Christ's sake. Just get rid of your friend, will you." The man's voice sounded anxious and something more urgent was clearly distracting him.

"Come on, Jonah. I've got a can of lager you can have. Let's go."

She tried to lead Jonah away, but he'd decided to be difficult, realising the crisis had passed.

"Ain't bloody good enough," Jonah shouted.

The man turned quickly, grasped Eileen's wrist and took the money from her. Jonah ducked behind Eileen as he realised the man was approaching him but, instead of hurting him, the man grabbed Jonah's coat and shoved the money into one of his pockets. Jonah backed away and put his hand in the pocket, shutting his fingers around it.

"Now, for Christ's sake, go away." The man shouted the final two words to make Jonah move, rather than stand arguing.

Almost immediately the door of the jewellers flew open and the men who had gone inside ran out. The last man was carrying a gun.

"Grab this and go." The man without the gun had two bags and threw one of them at the lookout.

The lookout tried to avoid Eileen's lumpy figure but cannoned into her as he rushed to get into the car. The force of the collision knocked Eileen over and the man fell on top of her, losing his grip on the bag he was holding. It landed at Jonah's feet and jewellery spilled out. Disentangling himself the man scrambled up. The jeweller's alarm was activated, and the car started moving.

"Get in," a voice shouted, "Leave the bag and get in."

The man did as he was told, and the car accelerated away. It was all over in a few seconds. Jonah bent down, picked up one of the pieces of jewellery that had fallen out of the bag and held it up, watching it sparkle in the sunlight.

"Give me that." The manager had heard the car draw away and had come out of the shop. He reached across and grabbed the piece of jewellery from Jonah's hand.

"Don't shout at him," an onlooker said. "If it hadn't been for him and the woman, you'd have lost the lot."

Two men helped Eileen to her feet, and she smoothed her skirt down. Jonah, bewildered, grinned at the various people closing-in round him, picked-up another piece of jewellery and held it out to show them. The police arrived almost immediately and pushed through the crowd.

"What are you doing here?" one of them asked, spotting Jonah. "Always around when there's trouble, you and your friends."

"On this occasion it appears that he and this lady impeded one of the robbers," the shop manager said, "And helped prevent the loss of some of the stolen items."

"That's right, ah 'elped save some of the jewellery." Jonah had had sufficient time to realise that he might benefit from the situation. He bent down, picked-up the dropped bag and clung to it, looking round at the people surrounding him and milking the moment for all it was worth.

"You'd better let me have that bag," the policeman held out his hand.

Jonah held on.

"The old boy deserves a reward," said a voice from the crowd, "The woman too. Bloody brave, both of them."

One of the policemen stepped forward and finally relieved Jonah of the bag, whilst the other moved the crowd back.

"I hear you were involved in this." A youngish man, tall and with a rather lived-in face, appeared. He spoke to Eileen. "I'm Iain. I'm a reporter with the local paper. Perhaps you can tell me what happened?"

Eileen told him what she had seen, and Iain made notes, whilst a cameraman looked round for suitable pictures. He called across, "The old guy holding out the bag will make a good shot, assuming the police will let him have the bag back for a few minutes."

"His name is Jonah," Eileen volunteered.

The policeman who'd recovered the bag from Jonah reluctantly let him have it back for the shot. "This'll make a superb front page," the photographer cleared a space and got Jonah and Eileen to pose together, then took the picture and returned the bag to the policeman. "And what a headline: 'LADY AND TRAMP FOIL ROBBERY'."

Eileen began to tell the reporter the story. The photographer interrupted her narration and took the reporter aside.

"The wino's being awkward," he said, "Wants a cigarette."

"Here," Iain produced a packet from his pocket, "See if he'll smoke these."

The photographer gave the cigarettes to Jonah whilst Iain continued to question Eileen. Jonah took one and dropped the packet containing the rest into his red bag. Somebody gave him a light and he inhaled deeply. He moved his head back and opened his mouth wide, letting the smoke escape gradually and curl in a cloud up into the air. He was smiling.

The photographer interrupted Iain again.

"He's asking for a drink now. Says thanks for the cigarettes but wants a drink before he'll co-operate. Says his nerves need calming."

"If we give him a drink, he won't remember anything, and we'll never get another picture." Iain took a banknote out of his wallet. "Tell him he can have this if he stands outside the shop with Eileen and smiles for us."

"Me name's Jonah," said Jonah. "Doesn't mean what people think. Fish spat 'im out again in the bible. Must 'ave been a proper reason."

"It spat him out because he had to go to Nineveh and tell them to mend their wicked ways, or God would destroy them," said the photographer. "And so, he did what he was told to. And the people in Nineveh wore sackcloth and ashes and repented. And the whole of Nineveh was saved. Now smile, like I've asked you to, and I'll give you this." He held-up the banknote Iain had given him.

"Somehow, I don't see him as a messenger of God," Iain said as he finished interviewing Eileen and wandered over. "But he takes a good picture."

"This was my Nin'veh"; Jonah hadn't caught the name properly and looked at the photographer for corroboration. The photographer nodded and gave him the banknote. Jonah took it and stuffed it in his pocket. "Sent here to save the jewellery, like the other Jonah saved Nin'veh," he looked again at the photographer to make sure he'd got the name right.

"Somebody's just told me the robber fell over Eileen here," Iain pointed at Eileen, "And they say the bag landed at your feet, the robbers fled, and you just picked the jewellery up."

"Deserve a bloody reward, ah do," Jonah ignored what the reporter had said. "Would've got away with everything if ah wasn't here. Bloody wrong if ah don't get a reward."

"Well, don't hold your breath," said the reporter. "It may not arrive until you're in heaven, drinking your unlimited supply of super strength lager and smoking the celestial cigarettes you've taken from the other angels."

Jonah disappeared for the next few days. Eileen looked out for him, but he didn't come to the shop. She guessed he must still have some of the money the photographer had handed him and didn't need to beg for booze or call round for cigarettes.

"Couldn't stand bein' pestered," he muttered when he finally turned up again.

"Busy drinking your way through that money the reporter gave you, more like," Eileen scolded him good-naturedly. "I thought you were going to cut down on the drinking."

"Man's gotta 'ave a last fling." Jonah grinned as she gave him some cigarettes.

"And if that's the truth then I must be the Queen of England," Eileen snapped back in mock disgust. "Still, you're a bit of a celebrity now," she held the local paper up so he could see his picture on the front page. "Did they give you a reward?"

"Not a bloody penny," Jonah shook his head and looked at the picture again. "But if ah 'adn't been there, they'd 'ave got away with the bloody lot. Should've left 'em to get on with it. Should've stayed inside the bloody fish instead of goin' to that Nin'veh place to save 'em."

It's Tough

It's tough on the street
When you ain't got enough
To pay for a bed,
End up sleeping out rough.
There's always the traffic
And feet passing by,
It's hard to nod off long
As hard as you try.
Then kids come along
And just for a laugh
Piss down as you lay there
To give you a 'bath'.
It's tough on the street
When you ain't got enough
To pay for a bed,
End up sleeping out rough.

Mike, Going Up

Down on the main road the early morning traffic was flowing into town. It was seven-thirty and by eight there would be a long slow line of vehicles filled with people going to work. Out of his lounge window Mike could see high autumn clouds stretching across the pale blue sky and there was a chill in the flat. He shivered slightly, partly because of the chill and partly because he was afraid of what lay ahead. He'd been out of work for nearly a month now and no longer felt part of the big outside world, the world of the people in the cars below.

He wondered whether the cat was around. Nobody knew who owned the cat, but everyone fed it from time to time. It had spent the summer laying in the window of the shop below, soaking up the sun and being stroked by shop assistants and children who'd come in from the street. Since he'd been out of work, Mike had fed the cat every day. The shop below had been extended at the back of the building and every morning the cat walked up the lean-to roof and through Mike's kitchen window to the food bowl he'd bought. "Lucky bugger," Mike thought ,"No worries. You just turn up and somebody feeds you."

This morning, though, the cat wasn't around. He turned on the radio, but the news had been the same for days and he switched it off again. The kettle boiled and he poured the water into the cafetiere, watching the brown liquid rise frothily up to the rim. As he carried it along the hall, making for the lounge, he heard a vacuum cleaner on the stairs outside. Curious, he unlocked the flat door and found Gill, the girl from the flat above, cleaning the worn stair carpet, her tight jeans showing off her neat figure and long legs.

"What are you doing?" he shouted.

"Sorry about the noise," she turned the cleaner off, "But I couldn't stand the dust any longer and thought I'd clean up before I left for work. Sorry if I woke you."

"No problem, I generally get up early," he waved her apology away, "Look, if you're in a hurry, leave the rest and I'll clean down to the ground floor later. I've got my own cleaner, just not very good at using it!"

"Really? Well, if you're sure, that'll be terrific." She looked at her watch, "God, is that the time? I must fly."

Mike checked the news, finished his second cup of coffee and went outside to clean the stairs. The cat still hadn't appeared by six in the evening, and he wondered if anything had happened to it. The doorbell interrupted his thoughts. It was Gill.

"The stairs are great." She smiled. "Thanks. Did it take long?"

"No, I had it done in no time. Look, I'm making a pot of tea, why don't you come in for a cup?" He grinned, "You must be exhausted after a hard day's work."

"Isn't that meant to be the woman's line?" she giggled slightly. "But yes, I'd love to."

She was easy to talk to and to look at, with high cheekbones and amber eyes softly framed by discreetly applied shadow. Her hair was glossy and dark, and she wore it in a bob, showing off her elegant neck and shoulders.

"How did you lose your job?" Her directness surprised him.

"Well, it all sounds a bit weak really," he replied. "I was a salesman and I thought I was doing well, but the manager told me I had a few problems inside the office. One woman was particularly difficult. I heard later she was rumoured to be having an affair with the manager, "

"Bad idea, upsetting the boss' mistress - unless you don't fancy staying around too long."

"Yes. But I did want to stay around, I just didn't know about the affair at the time and the woman was a liability, a total nightmare. The way she treated customers sometimes was appalling. And she wasn't much better with me or some of the other members of the sales team. It's all very depressing. Anyway, enough about my woes, what do you do with yourself?"

"I organise conferences, I've started-up my own business. I used to work for an events company, made some good contacts and decided I could do things better on my own. I'm organising a conference tomorrow, outside Renford. It's the reason I had to rush off this morning - to make sure all the arrangements were coming along as they should be."

"Renford's beautiful," he pictured the main street and the picture postcard square. "What sort of conference is it?"

"It's a sales conference. Right up your street, in fact. Look, if you're bored hanging about the flat, why don't you come along for the drive? You can help me cart some of the boxes and staging about and maybe you'll pick up a few names of people who might be useful."

"That'll be great. I could do with a day off from sitting in the flat, searching through the local 'positions vacant' columns."

"Fine, I'll call for you around seven-thirty." She got up to leave, "And thanks for the tea."

When she rang his doorbell the next morning the cat had still not re-appeared. They walked to her car together; it was large and black, with an untidy rear seat and packed boot.

"The conference details are in an orange folder," she nodded at the boxes of folders on the back seat, "You can take a look, if you can find it."

Mike found the folder and read quietly for a few minutes. His concentration was interrupted as Gill stamped on the brakes to avoid a ragged grey figure that lurched off the pavement.

"That's Jonah," Mike recognised the charcoal-coloured overcoat, tied with coarse string, and the red vinyl bag. "My mother works in a newsagent's and he's always trying to cadge cigarettes from her."

He hesitated before deciding to continue.

"The last time I saw him was the day I was fired. I was upset, popped into a pub for a few drinks and ended-up by elbowing a shop bloke in the face. It was an accident, although he thought I did it purposely. I met Jonah as I went into the shop, and I've had nightmares ever since in case he tells someone who I am."

"Do you make a habit of assaulting people?" Gill asked.

"No, of course not," he replied. "I dropped a loaf on the floor, and he suddenly appeared behind me and said I couldn't put it back on the shelf. I swung round, surprised he was there, and caught him in the face. I should have stayed and explained things when the police arrived, the guy's wife said she was going to call them, but I was scared and ran away instead."

"Open the glove compartment, Mike Tyson, and find the packet of mints I keep for car journeys." She smiled across at him. "And stop worrying so much; I can't recall seeing any 'Wanted' posters around town, with your face plastered all over them. Maybe they realised it was an accident when they'd had time to think about it."

Mike took out the mints, passed one to her, and sat back to enjoy the ride. Once they'd reached Renford, he picked-up the conference papers again, flicking through the delegate list. "That's a coincidence, you've got Rogers attending," he stabbed at the list of names with his finger, "He's the bastard who fired me, the one who's supposed to be having an affair with the woman I told you about."

"Good idea to keep away from him." Gill looked worried, "A confrontation is the last thing I need at the conference."

They arrived at the hotel early, and Mike helped to set-up the last pieces of staging and lay out the conference folders on the reception desk. Wanting to avoid meeting his ex-manager, he went into the restaurant and ordered a coffee. As soon as the opening address had finished, Gill quietly ushered him into the back of the hall and he spent the first few minutes looking for Rogers' immaculately groomed, grey hair. He found him sitting a few rows from the front. The session passed slowly, he'd heard most of the content before, and he left the final presentation early, anxious in case Rogers saw him. He decided to miss out on the afternoon presentations and, after lunch when the conference resumed, settled into a deep settee in the reception lounge, watching people come and go.

"Hey, the conference seems to be going ok," Gill joined him for a while, sounding excited as she sat down next to him. But the opening of the automatic entry doors and the appearance of a carefully made-up, middle-aged woman distracted him. She was carrying several bags and had clearly been on a shopping trip.

"That's her," Mike gave Gill a quiet nudge and whispered to her, "Mrs Serjeant, Rogers' mistress," he must have brought her with him."

"She's not bad for her age," Gill noted the immaculately presented hair and the full, but still firm figure, "She obviously takes a lot of care with her appearance."

"Don't stare, you'll draw attention to us," Mike whispered and looked down, pretending to be reading some of the Conference papers.

The woman picked up the room keys at reception and walked towards the lifts. One lift was already on the ground floor, and she entered it on her own. Mike stood up, so he could see the floor indicator, and noted the floor it went to, before returning to the reception area.

"Will you do something for me?" Mike asked. "Will you go and find out which room Rogers is staying-in? They're more likely to tell you as you're the conference organiser."

"Not if you're going to do anything stupid." Gill looked across at him unsure, concerned that nothing should happen to spoil the success of the event.

"No, I promise to behave. Scouts honour," he raised his fingers in a mock salute. "I just want to call her anonymously on the house phone – let her know she's been seen. It won't involve you; I promise."

Gill was reluctant, but did as she was asked, and passed the number to him. He waited a few minutes and then called on the house-phone. A woman's voice answered.

"Is that Mrs Serjeant?" Mike asked using her real name.

There was a pause before she replied.

"You must have the wrong number." She sounded hesitant, uncertain how to respond.

"I'm sorry, they told me this was Mrs Serjeant's room. My apologies for bothering you."

He replaced the handset and redialled, but this time there was no answer and he re-joined Gill on the settee.

"Satisfied?" she asked.

"Well, let's put it this way, I don't think tonight will be one of their more enjoyable nights together. At the very least, Rogers is likely to find her somewhat distracted."

"Look, the conference will be ending soon, I'd better get back." She finished her drink and got up. "I'll see you in about forty-five minutes."

After half an hour, the delegates began to emerge. Mike spotted the tall figure of Rogers without difficulty. He was talking to a group of other men and Mike walked across and held out his hand.

"Hi," he said, "Quite a coincidence meeting you again so soon."

"Er, yes," the other man shook his hand without enthusiasm. "What are you doing here, Mike?" He looked at his watch and continued speaking before Mike had a chance to answer. "I hope you don't think I'm being rude, but I must rush."

Mike watched as he walked across to the lifts and wondered what was going through the other man's mind. A lift bell rang and, when the doors opened Mrs Serjeant emerged, looking flustered.

"Jim," Mike could hear what she was saying and watched with amusement as she gripped Rogers' arm, "Somebody called the room and asked for me, they must know what's going…"

She stopped and stared as she saw Mike's smiling face. He turned away. Satisfied.

"You look pleased with yourself." Gill had finished for the day. "What's been going on?"

She ordered herself a coffee and they sat down together. Mike related his conversation with Rogers and the sudden emergence of Mrs Serjeant from the lift.

"I wonder what they'll do now?" He considered for a moment. "Go home? Brave it out? Find a new hotel?"

The coffee arrived accompanied by two large cream cakes. Gill took one and Mike took the other, bit a large piece out of his and ate contentedly.

"Mm. They've got nothing to worry about, but it's nice to know they can't be sure about that." He slid his finger along the edge of the cake and collected some cream that had squeezed out. "I've got a lot more important things to do than telling people about their passionate nights together - like getting another job for example."

"I might be able to help you there." Rogers' voice startled them. Neither of them had noticed him approach as they talked.

Gill looked up and was impressed by the man's expensive air: the grey hair without a strand out of place, the dark suit with a deliberately conspicuous tie, the beautifully manicured hands. Rogers had a natural elegance.

"May I sit down?" He did so without waiting for their answer. "I've got a friend who's looking for a good salesman, Mike," he paused, "I could get you an interview later this week, I think you're just the kind of young guy he's looking for - providing you undertake to keep quiet about what you've seen today. Both of you." He looked pointedly at Gill.

"Oh, come on. You fire me because your mistress doesn't like me and then you offer to use your influence to get me a job with someone else." Mike was angry but controlled his voice. "Do you really think you can play around with peoples' lives so easily?"

"Yes." Rogers smiled. "Most people are losers, but you don't have to be. It's 'make your mind up' time. There's nothing else on offer, take it or leave it."

"Mike isn't going to tell anybody about today anyway," Gill interrupted.

"I can't rely on that. He may change his mind tomorrow or the day after." The man leant forward. "But, if Mike gets this job, with my backing, there will be a continuing reason for his silence." He stood up. "Do you want the job, or not?"

"Yes," Mike stayed seated, "But because you owe me a job, not because of anything else."

"Look at it in any way you like. I'll be in touch." Rogers turned to Gill. "Nice meeting you; and well done with the conference." He bowed his head slightly and walked back towards the lifts.

Mike was poor company on the way back. His earlier good humour had been replaced by a sullen recognition that he had lost and been forced to accept Rogers' terms.

"Cheer up, at least it sounds as though you've got a new job." Gill accelerated past the car in front.

"I'll tell him where he can stick his bloody job. I'm buggered if I'll let him think he can buy me."

"Don't be so ridiculous. If you promise to go to the interview, I'll buy you a drink at the pub tonight." She stared ahead, apparently concentrating on the traffic. "Besides, he didn't have it all his own way, he had to accommodate you. Take the opportunity and, if you're successful, he won't be able to touch you."

"Ok, the drinks are on you." Mike smiled. "You're right, I'm broke, I need the job and I'm ready for a night out."

They were almost home when Mike recognised a familiar figure drinking on a roadside bench.

"Pull in, here," he pointed urgently at the kerb, "There's Jonah again. I want to see if he recognises me."

He jumped out of the car and walked across to the bench. Jonah was draining the remnants of a lager can, his head thrown backwards to enjoy the last few drops.

"Hi, how's it going?" Mike bent down so he was at Jonah's eye level.

Jonah put the can down and glared suspiciously at the younger man. "What you after?" Jonah's voice rose. "I ain't got nothing. Piss-off."

Mike stayed still, waiting for a sign of recognition.

"Can't spare a few pence for something to eat, can yer?" Jonah's voice adopted a more conciliatory tone. "Ah 'aven't eaten all day."

Mike had little money with him, but he gave Jonah a few coins from his pocket. Jonah took them and touched his forehead in acknowledgement. The lager finished, he searched in his red vinyl bag for another can.

"He didn't recognise me, didn't know who I was," Mike sounded excited as he got back into Gill's car, "I'll bet the guy in the shop wouldn't recognise me again after all this time, or his wife either. All I need now is for the cat to be there when we get back and everything will be alright with the world."

They parked the car and walked back to the flats. As he opened his front door, Gill pushed past him and went down the hall into the kitchen. Sitting on the windowsill was a small grey tabby cat. It stood up and stretched when it saw her, yowling to be let in. She opened the window and it brushed against her hand, purring as it stepped inside.

A Local Hero

"Christ, is that really you in there?" Iain stared at the puffy face in the bedroom mirror and examined the large bags under his eyes. "Always had baggy eyes," he muttered, "but the rest of me didn't look so gross."

'DRUNKEN REPORTER WAKES WITH MASSIVE HEADACHE', he could see the imaginary headline clearly. "Damn sight more interesting story than 'LOCAL MP PROMISES NEW DEVELOPMENT AND JOBS'," he said to himself, "Although it was pretty amusing when he got the bloody location wrong. Obviously knew very little about the project." He walked down the hall, pushed open the kitchen door and filled the kettle. Then looked round for the teapot.

The teapot was half full of water, with tea bags floating on the top. He poured the contents in the sink and picked the bags out from amongst the debris of mugs and spoons that had been left since the previous day.

"Must start washing-up before I go to bed," he made a mental note, "God, my head is killing me."

He filled a glass with water, then went to the bathroom and took a couple of aspirin from the packet in the cabinet. His head still aching, he went back to the kitchen to resume making his cup of tea.

The tea bags were not in the cupboard where he normally kept them. He lifted up yesterday's paper, but they weren't under there either. He found them behind a bag from the Chinese take-away, warmed the teapot and dropped a couple in.

"Morning, Iain." The voice startled him. "Feeling a bit fragile, are we? Can't say I feel in the pink myself."

"Christ, Andy, you gave me a shock. I'd forgotten you'd stayed."

"Now I could be offended by the implication that I'm unmemorable. But I've seen the pressures a local journalist works under. Covert meeting with a local government whistle-blower, after which you joined me for a pleasant hour or so in a wine bar, where we sank a few glasses of not very good house wine. Then on to cover the political and social event of the week at the City Hall, followed by a couple of beers in the pub opposite. We've got a right to feel a trifle jaded. And, on top of that, your sofa's not the most comfortable place for a good night's sleep."

"Can't remember much after the pub," Iain rinsed two of the less heavily soiled mugs and dried them on the dishcloth he found draped across the bread bin. "How did we get home?"

"Iain, Iain, what are we going to do with you?" Andy grinned. "After the pub was the best bit. You were magnificent."

"That's the line my women never use afterwards," Iain shook his head, "They don't even infer it with a heavy, drowsy expression. Don't tell me we picked up a couple of women and I missed out on my five minutes of triumph?"

"Better than that," Andy slapped him on the shoulder, making him pour tea over the counter instead of into the cup, "You spoiled the mad hatter's tea party. The MP and the Mayor, eating and drinking with all their friends in the parlour. I knew some of them at school and most of them are bastards." He spoke deliberately, his previous bantering tone gone.

Iain heard the change in Andy's voice and turned to look at his face.

"And, last night, you hit them where it hurts." The humour of the situation returned to Andy, and he began to smile. "Kicked them in their pretensions as they sat at their tables mixing with the local not so good and great. God, that was a sight for sore eyes."

"Shit. Jonah," Iain whispered. He remembered coming out of the pub and seeing Jonah in his charcoal-coloured coat, wrapped round with string; a dishevelled figure with his red vinyl bag and clanking tins of lager hanging from his hand, as he leaned against the sidewall of the City Hall. "Why the hell did you let me do it?"

He shut his eyes, recalling how he had gone back to let Jonah into the Hall through a side-door, telling him there was free booze inside. And he visualised Jonah's manic entry into the dinner and the anarchy that followed.

"Couldn't stop you. You told me to 'piss off' when I tried. Said it was something you had to do. You certainly know your way round that building. I was particularly impressed by the speed with which you got us back to the dining room gallery."

Iain recalled the chaos and anger that Jonah had caused, in mental technicolor. The ragged figure shouting and waving his fist at the men in black ties and the women in their cocktail dresses. Some guests had begun hollering back, standing-up and yelling for someone to remove him.

"One bloke was actually suggesting they hang Jonah from the town hall balcony." Andy relived the moment happily. "Pity it was all over so quickly. From the moment we left him in the corridor it was suspense all the way, like waiting for a time bomb to go off and not knowing whether we'd be far enough away to escape the blast. If we hadn't got to the gallery so quickly, we'd have missed the whole show." He chuckled. "For an old boy, living rough, he certainly handles himself well. Took three of them to get him out. You could hear him shouting all the way back down the corridor."

"Poor Jonah," Iain shook his head, "I shouldn't have let him in, even if I was out of my head. I used him."

"All you did was point him at a room full of booze and give him a packet of fags and a few quid into the bargain. Great theatre, he seemed to be enjoying himself as far as I could see. Everybody likes a chance to indulge their own paranoia and I guess Jonah is more paranoid than most." He took the cup Iain offered him and tried the tea. "Hot. Anyway, he could have gone straight back out the side exit if he'd wanted to."

"And then I filed my report." Iain got to the part that was really bothering him.

"And then, as you rightly say, you filed your report." Andy tried his tea again. "Not bad, better than you usually manage."

"The tea or the report?"

"The tea, though the report was a right corker. And I loved the headline, 'LOCAL COUNCILLORS ENTERTAINED BY DEVELOPER'. So well researched, too. I didn't realise you'd had time between the wine bar and the pub to verify what your 'unnamed source' had told you. Personally, I think they'll roast you crisper than the Sunday potatoes. They'll pull your skin off with pincers." Andy was obviously enjoying the rich images of torture.

"Oh, come on. It wasn't that bad." Iain tried to recall what he'd submitted. "I always cover myself. You know, 'allegations were made by someone close to the local Council that some Councillors had benefited from an expensive weekend away, ostensibly to gather more information about a proposed development before granting planning permission'."

"That's not quite how I recall it. It all sounded very cut and dried to me."

Iain decided that Andy had a definite sadistic streak.

"You can't expect too much equivocation after several glasses of wine and a couple of beers. Everything seems clearer, much more 'black and white' than it does later, when the alcohol wears off. It's asking too much of the old grey matter to take a balanced view." Andy tapped the side of his head and winced. "Haven't got any aspirin, have you?"

"Sorry, don't use the stuff." Iain lied with satisfaction, picturing the half-finished packet of tablets in the bathroom cabinet but deciding Andy deserved to suffer for a while longer. "If what I submitted was half as bad as you make it sound, the editor would never publish it."

"Well, it did surprise me, the way they seemed to accept what you said so uncritically. As I recall it, your precise words were 'It's front page' and then you did a passable imitation of a winning goal scorer and leapt around in the road a lot. Are you sure you haven't got any aspirin?"

Iain shook his head.

"Pity, I could really do with some. Where's the radio? Let's listen to the news," Andy suggested. "Maybe the local station has picked up some reports."

"It's over there," Iain waved vaguely at the mess on the worktop. "You'll have to tune it in, you've got about two minutes."

Andy swept aside some of the papers and bottles that littered the worktop, turned the radio on and tuned-in to the local station.

"The main local news this morning," announced the reader, "Centres on allegations that some local councillors accepted entertainment before approving plans for a new development. There was also uproar at the town hall when a drunken intruder broke into a dinner attended by the local MP, Mayor, Councillors and prominent local business-people."

"I can't bear to listen," said Iain and switched the radio off as the list of other stories followed.

"Well, you certainly surpassed yourself this time," Andy grinned happily. "Normally, you just report what happened - this time you can claim to have actually made the news."

"Piss-off, Andy. Your enjoyment is beginning to show too much. This could be really bad for me."

"How did you get to know Jonah?"

"Oh, he got in the way of a robbery, quite literally. Stumbled across a bag one of the thieves dropped as the guy ran out of the jeweller's shop and collided with a rather large woman. Thief dropped some of the jewellery right at his feet. Jonah was a local hero for a couple of days, captured the local imagination very briefly. We published a picture of him on the front page with the woman and some of the loot."

The telephone rang.

"Answer it," Iain said, "I don't feel up to it."

"Hello," Andy did as he was asked. "Who is it, please?" He mouthed the caller's name.

Iain shook his head.

"No, I'm sorry, he's not here at the moment. I'm a friend. Can I take a message, or will you call back? No, I'm not sure when he'll be back. Bye." He put the handset down.

"Oh God," Iain covered his face with his hands, "That's the editor. Did he say anything?"

"No. Wouldn't leave a message, but he sounded pretty anxious to contact you. Wants you to call him as soon as possible." Andy drank the last of his tea. "This could set off the biggest local legal frenzy for years. Solicitors will love it. Could be the equivalent of one of those old New York ticker tape receptions with writs flying everywhere."

"I doubt that," Iain tried to reassure himself, "The story's true. Everyone knows some of the Councillors have been wined and dined under the pretext of researching the development. They won't want it all brought out and examined in public. And it doesn't end there. There've been other suggestions of them enjoying themselves on public money. I filed a story some weeks back about a trip to the States to look at how transport issues were being handled. Two weeks away, five day's work and the rest spent sightseeing. All expenses paid."

"I never saw it published and if it's so widespread and such common knowledge, why hasn't anyone produced the evidence?" Andy frowned, and flinched as he felt another pain in his head, "Why haven't the Councillors been challenged already? And don't underestimate them, they may be bastards, but they're clever bastards. How do you think they got where they are?"

"God, you're enjoying this."

"No, believe me I'm not," Andy shook his head, "There's nothing better I'd like to see than the bastards having their balls crushed with the same jackboots they use on innocents like Jonah. The whole system's flawed. It's based on people wanting power, often for the right reasons at first, but then using it unscrupulously afterwards."

"That's not very original," said Iain, "Power tends to corrupt and absolute power tends to corrupt absolutely. Heard that theory somewhere before. Can't really see the editor buying it: 'ANDY SMITH, REVELATION ABOUT POWER'."

"Wish you could see your way to making another cup of tea," Andy emptied the remaining liquid from the bottom of his cup, ran it under the tap and put it back on the worktop.

"I can't bear this any longer. Here," Iain gave the box of tea bags to Andy, "Make yourself a cup. I'm going to get a paper and see what they've actually printed."

The telephone rang again.

"Do me a favour and answer it. Please." Iain thrust the handset at Andy and unlocked the front door.

Out in the street the traffic was building up as people drove into town to work. Across the road was the railway station and Iain decided to buy his paper from the station kiosk, rather than get it from the local newsagent, whom he knew and who always wanted to chat about the latest headlines. He waited for a gap in the traffic, walked to the centre of the road and waited again until the queue of vehicles stopped, and he could complete the crossing safely.

As he approached the kiosk, he could see the paper on display and read the headline: 'MAYOR INVOLVED IN CORRUPTION ROW'. He looked for his name below, but it wasn't there. He bought a copy, scanned the first paragraph and then rushed back to the flat.

Andy had put the radio on again and was pouring his second cup of tea in the kitchen.

"It's not my article," Iain shouted, " I'm safe." He threw the paper down on the worktop, in front of Andy.

"That's like disclaiming the credit for the Watergate story," Andy tasted the tea. "Not bad. Do you want another cup?"

"Five minutes ago, you were predicting I'd be ruined and have writs dropping out of the sky on me. Now you're telling me I should take the credit for the story."

"It does mention allegations that some Councillors have been taking unnecessary trips to exotic places," Andy read the article as he drank, "Must be that story you uncovered. And it does talk about planning permission for the development you heard about from your informant yesterday. Well, it may not be under your name but, call me psychic, it sounds as though you may have come up smelling of roses."

"Psychic?" I can think of a lot of names I'd call you first," said Iain. "You've had some real fun seeing me sweat this morning. So why the change of attitude?"

"Well, that call I took was from your editor. And, since then, there's been a news flash on the radio. The mayor's resigned and one or two other people are considering following him. Apparently, the Mayor's mistress," he paused for another sip of tea.

"Just get on with it," Iain shouted. "What about the Mayor's mistress and who is she anyway? I hadn't heard anything about the mayor having a mistress."

"No-one had. He'd kept it all well-hidden. Anyway, he managed to slip her onto that American trip, you mentioned. At the taxpayer's expense, of course."

"How was it all uncovered? Who blew the whistle on him?"

"Hell hath no fury like a woman scorned - it may not be a very original line, but, in this case, it's true. Your editor wants you to get an interview with the mayor's wife, soon to be the ex-Mrs Mayor. Seems she received an offer of a free seat on her husband's next trip from the airline he and his mistress flew with. The airline ran a loyalty programme and wrote to all the wives they thought had flown with their husbands."

"I guess she was somewhat surprised to find out about her trip."

"She and a few others, no doubt. Anyway, she confronted Mr Mayor when he got home. He confessed, and she went public."

"What about Jonah?" Iain asked. "Did the report say what happened to him after they threw him out of the City Hall?"

"They kept him overnight at the police station, apparently. Then released him this morning with a warning. Realised there was no point in doing anything more. At least he had a dry bed for the night."

"I still feel bad."

"You'll feel a damn sight worse if you don't get off to interview the soon-to-be ex-Mrs Mayor. And ring your editor. I'll let myself out." Andy reached into his pocket, "By the way, next time you see Jonah, give him this from me." He pressed a banknote into Iain's hand. "He deserves it after the show he put on."

"I'll tell him not to waste it on booze, shall I?" said Iain. "Warn him about the trouble it gets you into."

"You can try. Tell him it gives you a terrible head the next morning."

"Guess he knows that already." Iain grabbed his jacket.

"What sort of a person doesn't have aspirin around their flat?" Andy asked. "My head's really throbbing."

"Don't know." Iain stepped out of the front door and called back before he closed it. "Couldn't live without it myself. You'll find some in the bathroom cabinet. Make sure the door's locked when you leave."

Chris, The Storekeeper

"God, I thought it'd never finish," Andy picked up his lager from the bar and took a long drink, "Mmm, that's better. Saw you yawning at the start of the afternoon session. Not one of the most riveting conventions ever – but you might have waited a little longer before feigning sleep!"

"The room was too warm," Chris looked round to see if there was anyone who might be listening to their conversation, "And the speaker had nothing new to say – the whole thing was rather boring." He recalled fidgeting throughout the morning session and then, for what he hoped had been no more than a couple of minutes, falling asleep in the afternoon. He felt sick at the thought someone might have noticed and hold it against him in the future.

"Your round, I think," Andy's happy voice interrupted the morbidity of his thoughts. "Come on, lighten-up," he nudged Chris with his elbow, "And try not to doze off if I start boring you. The floor's a long way down from these bar stalls."

"I haven't finished this pint yet." Chris held his glass up, showing him the remaining lager, then put it back on the bar. "I can't drink as fast as you."

"Another one's not going to hurt you," Andy signalled to the barman, "Another pint for my friend and one for myself, please." He waited for the barman to bring the new drinks over, took a mouthful and put his glass back down. "So, what did you think of the questions at the end? Takes me back to see the bright young things vying for approval. And talking of approval," he dropped his voice, "It looks like we may be in luck. Don't turn round now, but the blonde at the table by the window keeps looking across. And her friend's quite attractive. We could be in for a good night."

Chris choked as his lager went down the wrong way and put his glass on the bar until he'd recovered from the accompanying coughing fit. "Look, it may be ok for you to pick-up women, you're on your own, but Sally's expecting me back home this evening."

"Sally won't mind if you're late. God, how long have you two been married? She'll probably enjoy an evening to herself. And, anyway, she can't expect you home early after the annual convention. If you're really worried give her a ring. Blame it on me, say I insisted you stayed."

Chris was pleased at the opportunity to let Andy do some drinking on his own and left the bar to make his call in private. Sally answered and listened silently as he told her he'd been caught up in the bar with Andy.

"Quite frankly, I couldn't care what you do, so long as it helps us get out of this pokey flat and miserable little shop. Why you decided to serve the district's entire population of alcoholics is beyond me. None of the bigger stores will let them in, so why should we? That Jonah was in here again today. He pulled out a pocketful of rubbish and left it all over the counter whilst he counted out the money to pay for those extra strong lagers he drinks. He kept asking why you weren't at work, as though you're a friend of his. It was embarrassing. I told him you were at an annual meeting - not that it's any of his business."

Chris pictured the scene as she spoke and smiled to himself. He could imagine Jonah standing there in his charcoal-coloured overcoat counting the money out slowly and pleased at the opportunity to speak to someone. And there was more than one till to pay at, so he probably wasn't holding anyone up. Sally just didn't like serving people like Jonah, but arguing with her about it was pointless; they'd said it all before. She blamed him for not having a better job, for being too soft with the staff and some of the customers, and for the position she found herself in. When she'd put the phone down, he made his way back to the bar.

"It's not often we get to meet like this, is it?" Andy was pleased that Chris was staying. "Come on, drink up and enjoy yourself - have a bit of fun for once. Work hard; play hard, that's my motto. Maurice, the old regional manager, was the one for that."

"But Maurice was fired for embezzlement, along with that other manager over at Berwick Street." Chris remembered Maurice well. He'd hoped for promotion in the fallout following the scandal, particularly as Andy, whom he'd known for years, had replaced Maurice and the Berwick Street store had needed a new manager. But, as usual, he'd been passed over. They always had a plausible excuse for giving the job to somebody else. He took a long draught of his lager and, as he put it back down, asked himself whether he was becoming cynical or was he just the hopeless failure that Sally believed him to be?

"What did you say?" Andy was distracted from the meaningful smiles he'd been sharing with the blonde woman by the window.

"Nothing." Chris was confused, surprised he'd expressed his thoughts loudly enough for Andy to hear.

"I thought you muttered something about being cynical," Andy prompted, "You must be one of the least cynical guys I know. Come-on, drink up and relax. Working every evening and balancing the day's takings over a cup of cocoa is hardly living in the fast lane. Time to get another couple of pints in."

"But I haven't started this one yet," Chris drained the glass in his hand and indicated the extra one standing on the counter.

"You'll catch-up. The evening's young." Andy turned and smiled at the blonde again. "Besides, I reckon that blonde's friend fancies you. She keeps looking over here as well."

Chris started on his next pint, not wanting to fall too far behind Andy, and ignored the mention of the blonde woman's friend. But as he worked his way through his new pint, he found himself looking across more frequently and the more he looked, the more attractive he began to find her.

She caught him staring and smiled.

"Well done, I told you she fancied you," Andy turned his back on the girls and talked confidentially to Chris, "Let's give it a minute or so and I'll wander over and ask if they'd like a drink. What do you think?"

" I really don't think I should stay," Chris finished his drink and made a last effort to assert reason over the effects of the alcohol he'd consumed. Or maybe it was a request for reassurance? At this point, he was unsure what his real motive for protesting was.

"Nonsense, you'll go back to Sally a different man." Andy lowered his voice; " Enjoy yourself, have a bit of fun, you don't have to do anything you don't feel right about. It's not obligatory to make love to a woman on a one-night stand."

As Chris looked-up again he noticed the blonde coming towards the bar and hissed a warning at Andy, in case she got within hearing range.

"Excuse me, please." The woman ignored a space further along the bar and stood next to Andy. "I'm sorry to crowd you like this, but we need some more drinks, and it gets so busy here."

"Feel free," Andy stood-up and moved his stool away to give her space at the bar, "But before you order anything, we were wondering whether you'd let us get the next round and, perhaps, come and join you?"

"Are you two guys on your own?" she asked.

"Yes, we've been to a convention all day and after eight hours non-stop lecturing we thought we deserved a drink and a bit of recreation."

"Your wives didn't come with you then?"

"No, I'm separated from mine and Chris here's a widower. By the way, my name's Andy."

"I'm Laura," she nodded at Chris and then pointed across to the table she was sitting at, "And my friend's name is Sarah. Mine's a rum and coke please, and Sarah's drinking white wine."

Whilst Andy bought the drinks Chris tried to adjust mentally to the sudden change in his marital status. He followed Andy as he walked across to the girls' table, carrying the drink he'd already started in one hand and a fresh one that Andy had ordered in the other.

Laura placed the white wine in front of her friend and introduced Chris and Andy to her. She pointed at the seat next to Sarah, indicating where Chris should sit.

"To us," she raised her glass, "Good to meet you both."

"Cheers." Andy responded whilst Chris was still trying to find space for his accumulated pints among the other glasses on the table.

Andy was at his most charming, flattering and amusing the women. Chris had little to say and noticed that Sarah was also quiet. Occasionally she would give him a smile. As he reached the end of his pint, Chris began to be obsessed by the desire to touch her and sat staring down at the table, imagining how soft her skin would be.

"A penny for your thoughts," Sarah caught his faraway look, "Who's the lucky lady?"

Andy heard what Sarah had said and paused his conversation with Laura. "You never know with Chris. Women rush to give widowers like him hot meals, sympathy and anything else they want." He laughed and turned back to Laura.

"How long ago did your wife die?"

Sarah spoke quietly and directly, confusing Chris, who found the question difficult to answer. But the way it was asked, the soft undertone and the hand stretched out and placed on his, was indescribably appealing and cried out for an honest answer. His instinctive reaction was to confess it had all been a lie, but he felt obliged to continue the deception. In a sense, Sally had died, certainly their marriage had. She seemed to have shrivelled-up inside, her lonely disaffection creating an impermeable barrier between them, making it impossible to communicate.

"It was some years ago now," he replied trying to recollect when things had finally gone wrong.

"Who's for another drink?" Andy and Laura had both emptied their glasses. "Same again?" Andy asked. The women both nodded. "Good. And what about you, Chris?"

"He hasn't started the last one yet." Sarah's hand was placed protectively over Chris's glass. "You mustn't keep forcing lager down him, he'll be asleep before you know it." She removed her hand from the glass, and it brushed gently against Chris' hand as she did so.

"Be a good mate and do the honours will you?" Andy handed Chris the money. "And just a half for me this time."

Chris went to the bar as he was asked. Behind him he could hear Laura and Sarah laughing and felt hopelessly inadequate, envying the ease with which Andy was directing events. Chris worked hard and long but the past ten years had been a waste of time. In another ten years he would still be the manager of the same small store, assuming they hadn't closed it. And, in the evenings, as he completed his paperwork, he would still feel the palpable and silent hostility of Sally as she sat watching television, furious at his failure to deliver the lifestyle she wanted.

The whole convention had been meaningless. There would be another one next year and another the year after and, with or without him, the central characters would continue debating and posturing in the same way they'd done during the day that had just finished. Sarah turned and looked towards the bar, smiling as she caught his eye. Chris wished again he'd never come out for a drink, that he'd gone home and was sitting there in the familiar, safe surroundings. He handed the barman the money and waited for the change.

"I'll take Laura's and mine," Sarah's voice startled him. She reached out and picked up the glasses. "You looked very cross standing here - what's the matter?"

"Nothing, nothing at all. I was just thinking about the convention."

"It must have been pretty bad, if it makes you scowl like that." She edged against his shoulder as she turned round to go back to the table.

Surprised, Chris was off balance and beer from Andy's glass slopped onto his shoe. Sarah led the way back, easing herself between two chairs. It was a manoeuvre that caused her to hold in her stomach and reveal her figure to its best advantage. Chris was distracted by what he saw, lost concentration and spilled more beer onto the carpet.

"God, half of it's evaporated," Andy said as Chris put the glass in front of him. "It's a good job you don't take your eye off the ball at work, or you could soon be back managing one of the local stores."

Chris froze mentally, and then sat down to cover his surprise, realising Andy had been inventing a new personality for him whilst he'd been at the bar. Not knowing what had been said, he had no idea about the role he now purportedly filled in life and smiled at Andy anxiously.

"Andy's been telling us what you do - it sounds terribly high powered," Laura added unhelpfully. "How do you cope with it all, especially since you've been on your own?" She raised her glass and started to drink.

Chris wasn't sure how he coped either. With Andy's talent for exaggeration, he might be almost anything. His mind flitted over the possibilities, ranging from manager of one of the larger stores through regional manager to managing director of the whole national organisation. He dismissed being managing director immediately, Andy would always want the top position for himself, he wouldn't be able to imagine it any other way. Chris took another mouthful of lager and decided wise and devoted assistant was the most likely answer.

"Laura's got to get home," Andy finished his half-pint and put his glass down on the table, "So I said I'd see her back – we thought we might take in a Chinese on the way; do you two fancy joining us?"

Chris realised from the flatness in Andy's voice and the fixed stare Andy was giving him, that he was expected to decline the offer and made the excuse that he'd rather stay.

"You're welcome to come Sarah." Laura's invitation sounded more positive, but pointedly in the singular.

Chris waited for Sarah's answer with a rising anticipation of rejection. He tried to look casual as he picked up his glass and took a large gulp, preparing himself to say 'goodbye'.

"I'm not very keen on Chinese." Sarah stayed sitting, making no attempt to move.

"Ok, but would you like us to drop you off at home, or would you prefer to stay here?" Laura asked.

Chris picked his glass up again, his desire and pride conflicted, preparing for Sarah to leave and to drink-up and go home on his own.

"I'd quite like another drink," Sarah looked at him. "What about you Chris?"

Chris finished his drink and almost grabbed at her glass in relief. "Why not, I don't often have an evening out. Same again?"

Sarah nodded.

"That's settled then," Laura picked-up her bag and stood-up, ready to leave.

"Sorry, you'll have to give me a moment," Andy pushed his chair back, "I need to visit the gents before we go."

Chris felt a sudden panic seeing him walk away, still not knowing what Andy had told the women about him. He ordered the drinks, gave the money to the barman, and hurried to the toilet.

"Who am I?" He asked as he stood next to Andy.

"That's a bloody funny question to ask a man when he's having a pee," Andy finished and went across to the hand basins. "Sounds more like the sort of question they discuss on late-night television programmes."

"No, you bloody idiot," Chris was no longer in control of what he was saying. "What else have you told them about me or what I do?"

"You're my deputy, my right-hand man," Andy flicked the excess water off his hands and placed them under the drier, "Couldn't do it all without your help, you know."

"Couldn't do what?" Chris's voice was sounding higher as his anxiety increased.

"Do the job I do; I've told the truth about myself," Andy patted Chris on the shoulder, "But I did embellish things a little as far as you're concerned, so congratulations, you've been promoted to deputy area manager – but only for tonight."

" What?" Chris tried to come to terms with the idea as the doubts crept in. "How can you possibly expect them to believe that?"

"Just act the part for Christ's sake, you know more about the business than she does, so she's unlikely to catch you out." Andy took a last look in the mirror, checking his hair before going back out. "Besides, they're no different from us - just out for a bit of fun. The truth is not really that important on a one-night stand."

"But..." Chris started to speak.

"But nothing. You've got Sarah just where you want her - and, looked at the other way round, she's got you. It's a two-way game, and you've got to have more confidence in yourself." Andy paused, "I was worried you'd give the game away, but you've kept your end up well. We'll have to go out again, we don't make a bad team."

"That's crazy, I'm bloody married," Chris protested.

"What difference does that make?" Andy opened the gents' door to leave, "So was I once. Remember, it's only a matter of not asking too many questions. She won't ask and neither must you. And tomorrow you'll be back with Sally in the store, blaming it all on the drink and promising yourself it will never happen again."

Laura was waiting in the entrance to the bar and when she and Andy left, Chris collected the drinks he'd bought from the bar and took them back to the table.

"To us," Sarah raised her glass and tapped it against his, and Chris noticed she was slurring slightly, her lack of control adding a sense of vulnerability that he found attractive.

"So, tell me more about yourself. All I know so far is your name is Sarah and you drink white wine."

"Oh, I'm not very interesting. Married young and divorced a couple of years later. Big mistake, he was a shit - it's a familiar story." Sarah finished her drink. "Look, why don't we go round to my place. It's not far and I've got a couple of cans of lager in the fridge. They've been there since Christmas - there's not been much demand for them recently."

"Cans of lager will keep, I think I've had enough already." Chris put his glass down and stood up. "Mind you, a cup of coffee wouldn't go amiss."

"Ok, you're on," Sarah held out her hand and he helped her up from her chair. "Have you got a car?"

"Yes, it's in the carpark, but I'd rather leave it there and come back for it tomorrow. We'll take a taxi, there's a rank in front of the station."

As they walked, she put her arm in his and, when he looked down, she smiled and rested her head briefly against his shoulder. They walked slowly, mainly silent, just enjoying each other's company as they idled past the rows of old redbrick houses and small street-level shops. After a while, it occurred to Chris that somebody might recognise him. It was not a part of town that he normally visited but there was always the chance that someone might drive past.

"Is there a short cut to the station?" he asked.

"We'll turn down the next street, it bends later on and runs alongside the high wall bordering the railway line. There's a Church and an old building with a faded sign, somebody or other's commercial hotel or something. I used to live round here when I was a kid."

"Where do you live now?" Chris was beginning to feel more confident and able to talk more freely now they were on a quieter road. And Sarah seemed to like him, even if Sally no longer cared.

"Molesey," she said.

"Where?" He realised the word had escaped too vehemently, betraying the agitation he felt.

" Molesey," she repeated, "it's about two miles away, on the other side of the river."

Chris knew where Molesey was, he could walk there in ten minutes from his store. She might just as well have lived in the next street.

Where do you live?" Sarah asked.

Chris thought quickly. "Millington" it was a small town ten miles away. Chris had worked there once and knew it well. More importantly it was sufficiently distant to deter any further conversation.

"Oh, that's quite a distance away." She sounded disappointed. "I thought you might live round here".

Chris wanted to tell her the truth, but it was too late. The lies had gone too far and at a time when he should have been enjoying himself, he was feeling distracted by his rapidly increasing sense of guilt.

She reached up and kissed his cheek as they strolled. There was a small alleyway a few yards ahead and, as they reached it, she pulled him inside and kissed him again, but this time the kiss was more passionate.

"If you live so far away, we'd better enjoy ourselves whilst we can," she murmured, and gave him a small, teasing kiss on his neck.

He placed his hands against her sides and stroked her breasts delicately with his thumbs. Sarah looked up at him for a moment, kissed him again, and then turned away and led him out of the alley.

"Come on, let's go." She took his arm and they emerged back onto the street. "I remember disappearing down these dark alleys when I was a kid. It's one of the compensations of getting a bit older, at least you can take your time undisturbed, in the comfort of your own home."

In the taxi she sat tight against him, her fingers resting on his thigh. Chris didn't recognise the taxi-driver and hoped the driver hadn't recognised him - so many people passed through the store. He was torn between peering at the man and turning away as he paid the fare.

"Which is your place?" he asked.

They were standing outside one of the old red brick buildings with a trendy looking craft shop on the ground floor and flats above, a solid but decaying symbol of the urban middle-class that had occupied the area nearly a century earlier. Sarah pointed to a large window above the craft shop and led him towards the passage that ran to the rear of the buildings and the door of her flat.

"I've got my torch somewhere." She rummaged through her bag trying to find it.

"You don't need a torch tonight." Chris stopped as they stepped into the darkness and tried to kiss her, but she continued searching for the torch.

"It will only take a moment, we've got the whole night ahead," Sarah whispered as though she was afraid of being overheard, "It's just in case there are winos in the alley. We get a lot of them dossing down for the night in summer, and they get very aggressive if you tread on them." She giggled, found the torch and placed it in his hand, "Here, put it in one of your pockets so we can find it quickly."

He took it from her but, instead of walking on, she began to undo the buttons on his shirt, kissing his chest and pulling him tightly against her. He could think only of laying next to her, her skin against his, and of the complete concentration of feeling when they finally came together.

"I want you, let's go inside." Sarah took his hand and started along the passage.

They'd only gone a few paces when she stumbled. He stopped her from falling but, as she regained her balance, he heard a stream of obscenities coming out of the darkness.

"What's happening?" He held her tighter, anxious to protect her.

"Put the torch on, put the torch on." He could hear the panic in her voice, "There's a wino down here. He's got his arm round my leg."

"Get your hands off her," Chris shouted at the unseen owner of the arm, grabbed the torch from his pocket and pointed it down towards Sarah's feet. To his horror, the beam revealed the face of Jonah; eyes screwed up trying to see beyond the light that was dazzling him.

"Do something Chris. Tell him to let go of me."

He could feel Sarah trying to free her leg and get away from the person she was entangled with, but he was paralysed for a moment, unnerved by seeing Jonah there.

"Chris, is that you Chris?" Jonah had disentangled himself from Sarah's leg and was shielding his eyes with his hand. "Your missus said you was at some meeting all day".

"Move past him," Chris urged Sarah to go ahead, using the torch to help her avoid a second form that lay supine across the passageway.

"I thought you said you were a widower," Sarah reached out and took the torch and shone it in his face.

"'Tis you Chris, what you doing here?" Jonah could see Chris clearly now, illuminated in the darkness.

"Yes, what are you doing, Chris?" She mocked him quietly, whispering so that only he could hear. "At least you told me your real name. Was anything else true?"

"I wanted to tell you the truth earlier, but I was afraid in case it spoilt the evening." He raised his voice. "Sorry Jonah, I didn't recognise you. I was at a meeting, and they asked me to see this lady home. She's one of the other delegates."

Sarah pulled him round the corner of the building. "Listen, if you think you can disappear without an explanation, you're bloody mistaken. Besides... " She kissed him lightly on the neck.

"We can't. I've got to get back. Jonah comes in the store sometimes, for his booze. He knows me." The words were tumbling out of his mouth, and he stopped for a moment, trying to decide what he wanted to say. She waited quietly. "Ok, look, I really enjoyed this evening, I haven't felt this way with a woman for years. My wife and I don't get on anymore, I guess we both stay together because neither of us has anything better to leave for. She may not be dead, but the marriage is. I know that's an old line, but, in this case, it's true." He felt himself blushing, embarrassed by the emotion he was expressing.

"Ssh." She put a finger on his lips. "Kiss me again - just one more time. Then you can go home."

He did as she told him, prolonging the kiss and the closeness of her body. He stepped back slowly wanting to stay but knowing he had to go.

"Give me your 'phone," she held out her hand and saved her number amongst his contacts. "Call me when you get a chance. You owe me after cutting the evening short like this. I'm in there under the name Wright– it's a common enough name, and as long as you remember the flying brothers, you can't forget it."

"It's not easy. I've never had an affair." Chris was agitated, wanting to stay but back along the passageway he heard Jonah moaning and the noise overcame his inertia.

"Call me," she called after him. "Do something to please yourself for once - and bugger everyone else."

Ray's Lad

Shambling along in the city centre, Jonah kept muttering a song. Wrapped-up in the tune and oblivious to the people around him, he tried to recall the words to missing verses. He remembered the chorus, knew the story the song told and felt the emotion it contained. But the forgotten words wouldn't come back, so he hummed the gaps and repeated the chorus over and over again.

He could see the song's characters in his mind; searching for each other, meeting and then in the final verse, separated by events and wondering what the other was doing whilst they were parted. Sightless as far as the street was concerned, he bumped shoulders with people trying to avoid him as they flowed in the opposite direction.

"Watch where you're bloody going," a man responded angrily to the oblivious tramp.

But Jonah wasn't concentrating on where he was going. And the angry pushes and protests were not enough to distract him as he kept shambling towards the riverbank where he knew he would find some of his friends – drinking their booze under one of the trees. As he reached the river, he could see Mac and Ray sitting on the side further from him. So, he crossed the bridge, climbed down the steps and walked along the bank.

Mac was talking as Jonah sat himself down. "I 'ad an old uncle who used to say, 'Women are cruel, deceitful and bloody unkind'."

"And 'e wasn't far wrong there," Ray took a swig from his can of cider before continuing, "It was me wife that got me thrown out of me 'ouse. I 'ad it when I met her – she 'ad nothin'. Was living in a room in someone's flat. 'Ad nothin'." He shook his head as he reflected on the injustice of it all.

"'Ow'd she get the 'ouse, then?" Mac asked, "If it were yours in the first place?"

"It was the bloody court," Ray said. "We 'ad a lad and she reckoned she needed the place so 'e 'ad a roof over 'is 'ead. Couldn't believe it when the Court chucked me out on the street. Now it was me that was left with nothin'. Friends put me up for a bit, but I couldn't sleep on their sofas forever. Then I lost me job and the rest is 'istory." He raised his can, saluting his story, and took another swig.

"Bloody cruel," Mac said, "What about the lad?"

"Used to see 'im when I could," Ray said, "But it was difficult. I 'ad no money, what with the maintenance they made me pay. And I 'ad nowhere to take 'im. And then I lost me job and she moves this new guy into the 'ouse. After that she said the lad didn't wanna see me no more. Broke me, that did. Only thing I 'ad left was me friend 'ere." He tapped his can.

"D'yer reckon she was seeing the new guy before she 'ad you chucked out?" Mac asked.

"Dunno, no way of finding out," Ray shrugged his shoulders. "Flash bastard, 'e was."

Jonah reached in his bag and took out a can of extra strong lager. He pulled the tab and took a mouthful before speaking. "Where's yer lad now?" he asked.

"Dunno," Ray shrugged his shoulders again, "'E must've left school by now. Be good to know 'e was ok."

"Never 'ad no kids meself," Jonah said, "Bloody glad I didn't, seeing 'ow things bloody turned out." He took out a packet of papers and a tin of tobacco he'd recovered from discarded cigarette butts and made himself a roll-up. "Got no family, nothin'."

The three of them sat there, silently, considering the iniquities they'd been discussing.

"Why 'aven't you tried to see 'im?" It was Mac who finally broke the silence.

"I did," Ray took another swig of cider, "Went round to 'is school and tried to talk to 'im one dinner time – but 'e ran away and me wife said I'd scared 'im. Said she'd take me back to court if I tried to see 'im again."

"Don't 'ave much bloody luck, do you?" Jonah shook his head.

"No man 'as any fuckin' luck with the bloody Courts," Ray drained his can and threw it down, "We're second-class bloody citizens, as far as they're concerned. There's no bloody justice if you're a bloke."

Each of them nodded, agreeing. Then Ray lay back using his bag as a pillow and, after a couple of minutes, started snoring gently.

"Ah'm gonna carry on inter town," Jonah finished his can, "See if ah can cadge any money. Getting' short of booze." He climbed to his feet with difficulty and walked back along the riverbank towards the city centre. On the way, he found a newspaper stuffed in a waste bin, extracted it and took it with him, deciding it might be useful to sit on later.

"'Aven't eaten all day, can yer spare some change?" He stood outside a supermarket and held his hand out as people entered.

One woman bought him a bacon roll and some coffee, refusing to give him money to spend on booze. Jonah thanked her, ate the roll and longed for a lager instead. He continued begging until a younger man walked-up and started talking to him. The man looked familiar, fair haired and taller than Jonah, and Jonah tried to remember where he'd seen him before.

"You're Jonah, aren't you?" the man said.

Jonah wasn't used to people calling him by his name and felt uneasy. "'Oo's askin?" He stared, still trying to place the man's face.

"Well, there's gratitude for you. I make you a hero on the front page of the local paper for stopping a robbery and then introduce you to local high society at the City Hall – and you can't remember who I am!"

The mention of the City Hall prompted Jonah's memory, "You're the bastard what got me banged-up for a night! Told me there was free booze and let me in the door. All those bastards sitting there, drinking their fancy wines an' eatin' their posh dinners. Police took me to bloody jail." He waved the man away. "Piss off."

"I reckon I did you a favour," the man stayed standing in front of him, "At least you had a dry place to sleep for the night and a free cup of tea in the morning before they let you go." He grinned, "Now I'm offering you the opportunity to do someone else a big favour – and do yourself one at the same time."

Jonah felt unsure, "What've ah gotta do?" he asked.

"It's nothing difficult," the man said, "All I want is a little information."

"What information?"

"Tell me if you know a guy called Ray. And, if you do, tell me where I can find him."

"Why d'yer want to know? What yer going to do to 'im?" Jonah asked.

"I'm not going to do anything to him," the man said, "In fact I might have some really good news for him, something that could be a big help"

"What sort've good news?" Jonah was still suspicious, still unsure whether he should tell the man anything

"I can't tell you that, I need to talk to him personally," the man smiled, "But I promise you he'll be pleased to hear what I've got to say."

"And what's in it fer me?"

The man took out his wallet and held out a bank note. "A few cans of that super strength lager you drink."

Jonah reached-up to take the note, but the man moved it away. "Sorry, but I need the information first. You'll get it when you tell me where I can find Ray."

Jonah looked at the note, calculating how much booze it would buy. "'Ain't enough, won't buy me any baccy – like a smoke with me booze."

"You drive a hard bargain," the man said and took another note out of his pocket. "Will that be enough?"

"'E was back on the riverbank," Jonah reached out again, "Near the bloody bridge when ah last see 'im, couple of 'ours ago."

"And how will I recognise him?" the man asked, still holding the note out of Jonah's reach, "I've not talked to him before."

"Got red 'air," said Jonah. "Red 'air and a blue jacket."

"Thanks," the man gave Jonah the notes and turned away. "Oh, I almost forgot," and he took another note out of his wallet, "Friend of mine enjoyed your performance at the City Hall so much, he asked me to give you this the next time I saw you. So maybe it wasn't such a bad evening."

Jonah hadn't seen so much money in years, grabbed the extra note and shoved it into the pocket of his coat with the previous two. Happy he had enough to pay for the hostel that night as well and buy lager and tobacco, he gathered his belongings together. As he picked up the paper he'd found, a lottery ticket fell out from between the pages, and he scrambled to pick it up before it was blown away. He didn't bother to read the paper's headline, 'Local Lad James Wallace Wins TV Talent Show'.

The man drove off in the direction of the bridge whilst Jonah shoved the ticket into his pocket along with the money he'd been given and then started walking in the direction of the small store where he bought his booze. He bought a six-pack of lager and treated himself to a packet of tobacco. Outside the shop he hesitated, unsure which way to go. The cans in his red bag clanked with an insistence he found difficult to ignore and he longed for a smoke. He decided to find a bench in a small park, a place where he'd be unlikely to be moved-on and could relax for the afternoon.

"Jonah, it's bloody Jonah," a voice rang out across the park as he entered. He turned and saw Ray and Mac, beckoning him over. They were sprawled on a bench drinking, legs stretched out in front of them and cans of booze in their hands.

"'Ow'd it go in town?" Ray asked.

"OK," Jonah sat on the bench next to them, reached for a can from his bag, and put his finger through the pull. It opened with a satisfying fizz. He put it to his lips and took a couple of gulps.

"'Ow much did yer scrounge?"

"Enough," Jonah said, not wanting to tell them about the amount of money he'd been given or why. He took another gulp from the can, opened the tobacco and rolled himself a fag, then lit it and inhaled contentedly.

"Must 'ave done ok," Mac said, "Bought 'imself some baccy as well as the booze. 'Ere, give us a drag," he held his hand out.

Jonah ignored the hand and took another drag himself, wondering whether to let Ray know someone was looking for him. The man had said it would be good news, so he decided to tell him. "Bloke was looking for you," he pointed towards Ray, cigarette clenched between his fingers.

"'Oo was 'e?" Ray asked

"Bloke, from the local paper," Jonah replied.

"Don't know anybody from the paper," Ray heaved himself up on the bench and turned towards Jonah, concerned that someone was looking for him. "What did yer tell 'im?"

"Sent 'im down to the riverbank, must 'ave missed you. Prob'ly still looking. 'Ad a car. Small red un." Jonah took another gulp from the can and dragged deeply on his fag.

"What did 'e want?"

"Dunno," Jonah was enjoying Ray's discomfort, "Didn't say an' ah didn't bloody ask."

"Maybe 'e wants to tell you, you won the bloody lottery," Mac said.

"No chance," said Ray, "Can't win if you don't buy a bloody ticket. And with my bloody luck I wouldn't win even if I 'ad!"

Jonah was about to argue the point, remembering he'd found the lottery ticket that currently lay scrunched-up in his pocket. But then he decided to say nothing – inwardly cursing himself for forgetting to get the ticket checked in the store.

"What's this bloke look like?" Ray asked.

"Light 'air," Jonah said, "Tallish."

"Could be anyone," Ray replied, "Fat bloody 'elp that is. Why the 'ell did you tell 'im you knew me?"

"Why you worried?" Jonah didn't want to divulge the money he'd taken. "What you done?"

"Nothin'," Ray couldn't think why anyone would be looking for him but began to worry that the man Jonah had been talking to might not be from the local paper. "Better move on," he grabbed his bag, and started preparing to leave. "Need to get away from 'ere if I'm going to avoid 'im. S'posin' 'e followed you?" He looked accusingly at Jonah.

......

There was no sign of Ray at the riverbank and the man walked back to his car. As he got in, his 'phone rang.

"Hi, Iain, great headline about that kid Wallace," Iain smiled recognising his friend Andy's voice. "Just heard on the news that the tv talent show people have offered to put his dad through rehab if anyone can find him. Typical PR stunt! Guess you need to get to him first if you're going to get an exclusive."

"Easier said, than done," Iain replied. "Met up with Jonah and he sent me down to the river, but Ray had moved on. By the way, I gave Jonah that money you gave me for him. Didn't ask me to pass on his thanks, just grabbed it. He's probably drunk it by now. Must be feeling quite flush with the cash I gave him for information."

"Bloody ingrate," Andy laughed down the 'phone, "There's a small park near the town centre, I've seen some of the winos in there – might be worth going there and taking a look."

"Thanks for the tip. I'm on my way now." Iain ended the call and drove to the park. When he got there, he looked for someone who resembled Jonah's description of Ray. At first, he couldn't see anyone but kept walking until he saw Jonah sat on one of the benches. He waved at Jonah and called out as he approached.

Jonah looked-up and then shouted at Ray, who was still sitting with Mac gathering his things together. "That's 'im, the bloke 'oo asked me about you," he pointed at Iain.

Iain walked towards Ray, recognising him from Jonah's description. But Ray had heard Jonah shouting and, when he saw Iain approaching, got up and began to hurry out of the park and away from his pursuer. Iain chased after him, closing on him as he reached the entrance and shouting at him to stop.

The shouting only panicked Ray further. "I ain't done nothing, bloody leave me alone," he turned and yelled at Iain, before running out into the road as he tried to escape.

"It's about your lad," Iain shouted, waving him back, "He's just become famous!"

Iain heard the screaming tyres of an oncoming van. Then he heard a dull thud and Ray's scream as the van struck him. When he reached the road, Ray was laying on his side, trying to get back up. The driver was climbing out of the van shouting, "He just ran out in front of me!"

......

"Bloody genius, you've done it again," Andy was beaming over his pint as they sat outside the pub, drinking. "Not content with reporting the news, you have to go and make it!" He pointed at the front page of the newspaper he was holding. "You don't just find a new tv celebrity's long-lost dad, you chase him into the path of an oncoming van! God, you couldn't make it up!"

"Turned out ok, though, as I was the first to tell young James Wallace his dad had been found and was there at A&E when they made their touching reunion. Seems young James had wanted to contact Ray for some time but didn't know where to find him. Got the whole bloody story and we've sold it on, with exclusive photos, of course, to the tabloids."

Andy nudged his arm and pointed down the street. Iain looked round and saw Jonah shambling along towards them. As Jonah approached, he held-up Andy's newspaper, and pointed at the headline.

"Great news about your mate, Jonah. Lucky day for Ray."

"Getting bloody run over don't seem lucky to me," Jonah squinted at the page, trying to read the story Iain was pointing at. "Wouldn't 'ave 'appened if you 'adn't bin chasing 'im."

"Ray's fine, just a few bruises that's all. They let him out of hospital this morning," Iain put the paper down. "I was trying to talk to him, to tell him his son had won a tv talent show and had told the judges that the thing he most wanted was to find his dad."

"I can hear the audience ah-ing now," Andy said, "Women crying, guys hollering – as I said before, great PR message."

"You're a cynical bastard," Iain looked across the table and shook his head at Andy.

"Got some money fer a drink?" Jonah asked, pointing at Iain's glass.

Iain took a note out of his wallet and handed it to Jonah, "Here, and don't think you're getting any more." .

Jonah grabbed the note and put it in his pocket. "'Aven't seen Ray since, when's 'e coming back?"

"Don't suppose he will be coming back. The tv company are paying for him to go to a clinic and dry out, and the son looks like he's going to be mega wealthy and says he's going to make it up to Ray for all the years they've lost."

"'E'll be back, difficult to let go of yer best friend." Jonah jangled the cans in his bag. "Besides, if we'd been born lucky, none of us would've ended up where we 'ave."

As Jonah walked off, he kept his fingers wrapped tightly around the bank note in his pocket and felt the lottery ticket against the back of his hand. It reminded him that he needed to get it checked. "Maybe, my lucky day, too," he muttered, and started off along the street making for the tobacconist near the bus station carpark, where his friend Eileen worked. He handed the ticket to her to check the numbers.

"Congratulations, you've won £25, Jonah." She took the money from the till and gave it to him.

"That all?" Jonah asked.

"Be grateful, it's better than nothing," Eileen said, "better than getting run over."

Jonah shook his head, unsure, thinking about Ray and his son.

Sarah's Dilemma

Sarah picked-up the 'phone and recognised Chris' number. There was a brief silence and then a whispered 'hi' from the other end of the line. She'd been waiting for him to call to confirm the arrangements for the following evening, but his call had come later than she'd expected.

"Hi, I don't normally talk to strange men on the 'phone but, in your case, I'll make an exception - as long as you talk up so I can hear you." She giggled, teasing him and knowing he was afraid of being heard by his wife when he called.

"I'm sorry, it's been difficult to call, and I haven't got long." Chris spoke softly and urgently, constantly checking the door to make sure it was closed and listening for sounds on the stairs. "Are you still OK for tomorrow?"

"Yes, I'll meet you outside at eight," she whispered back. "What disguise will you be wearing? Will it be the grey mac, drawn up tightly round your neck and the trilby pulled down over your shades? Or are you going to wear something really anonymous, like a Father Christmas suit? They're all the fashion this summer."

"Look it's not easy," he began and then stopped because he thought he'd heard something.

"It's not easy for me either, Chris. It's difficult to contact you even if I need to. I always have to wait for you to call me." Her voice became more serious. "I wouldn't know if you'd died, until I read about it in the obituaries."

"Knowing the way my wife feels, she'd probably hire a plane and fly the news across the city on a celebratory banner." He heard his wife's voice calling him, "Look I've got to go, I'll see you tomorrow."

He arrived slightly late. She was looking in the window of the shop beneath her flat. It sold mugs, candles and craft items, things that were popular with students and young couples who wanted something distinctive. He pulled into the kerb and smiled as she got into the car.

"I like the shirt." She kissed him on the cheek. "Where to driver?"

"I thought we'd try that little pub on the Downs," he looked over his shoulder and pulled away, "And thanks for the shirt. Sally says it would look great - on a guy in his twenties."

"Meow," she ruffled his hair, "I've told you several times you should stop wearing clothes your father would have worn. You look great in more modern gear although you'd look even better if you lost some of this," she tapped his small paunch. " You wouldn't look a day over 50 if you slimmed a bit."

"Great, you're doing wonders for my self-esteem. So, I'm overweight and look middle-aged! Why bother going out with me at all?"

"Because," she paused for effect, "Because … Just give me a few minutes and I'll think of something! And by the way, you need some new shoes."

"I like these shoes, what's wrong with them?"

"We've only got an evening, we'll talk about it again when we've got more time! Let's talk about something less complex." She screwed her face up, pretending to think, "What's your view on quantum physics."

They drove out of the city, passing through long rows of older terraced houses, their doors opening directly onto the streets. And then, as they approached the outskirts, the houses became more modern, giving way to large commercial estates with factories and superstores on the other side of the ring road. Beyond the factories were trees and hedges and less frequent houses, each standing in its own generous plot of land. And, in the distance, they could see the Downs, high bare hills, sloping upwards in elegant curves from the valley below. As the car started to climb, the temperature fell slightly.

"I love it up here," Chris sighed contentedly, "When I'm up here, I forget the shop and Sally, it all seems light-years away."

"They're never far from me." She patted his leg. "The shop - or your wife."

"That bloody shop is at the root of most things." He revved hard and put the car into a lower gear. "It's partly why our marriage went wrong - that and not having children. Sally feels like I betrayed her."

"I went to the shop once, when I knew you wouldn't be there. I wanted to see what Sally looked like. She's still attractive."

"Why didn't you say something before?" Chris glanced across at her.

"Because I didn't want you to be worried or think I was crowding you too early in our relationship."

Chris smiled and shook his head. "When we married, Sally had big hopes for the future, thought everything would just fall into place, and when it didn't, she blamed me. If I'd been promoted, got a bigger store and job, she'd have been able to hold her head higher amongst her friends – although there'd still be the issue of not having kids. She's a few years older than me, and I guess it's probably getting rather late now."

"Supposing she got pregnant, would you still want kids?" Sarah's voice changed as she asked the question.

"No," Chris' response was immediate, "It would just imprison us in an already unhappy relationship. It might have been different if I'd been more successful, but I haven't."

"If you'd been more successful, we mightn't have met." She leaned across and put her head briefly against his shoulder. "Look at me as a reward for failure – I don't care what you have or haven't done. These last few months have been great - thanks partly to your grey-coated friend. If I hadn't stumbled over him, stretched out for the night in the alleyway by the flat, we might never have seen each other again. God, he scared me when I felt his arm round my leg."

"I don't suppose people trample across him every day," Chris smiled as he remembered seeing Jonah's unshaven face, and his eyes screwed-up in the torchlight. "People normally give him as wide a berth as possible. And imagine how I felt. Jonah often comes into the shop to buy his booze and he could easily have said something in front of Sally. It would have been a bit difficult explaining why I was in a dark alleyway with you when I was meant to be at the company convention chatting-up the regional manager."

"But he never did say anything?"

"No." Chris shook his head, "He must have forgotten."

"Well, he spoke very eloquently that night in the alleyway. Told me exactly where I stood, and about the married man I was with." Sarah looked over and smiled, "I still see him sometimes, with his coat tied round with string and his red shopping bag almost scraping the pavement."

"I was surprised you wanted to see me again," Chris thought back to the chaotic few moments that night, when he'd been forced to confess to the lies he'd told her earlier.

"It surprised me too. I've had a couple of encounters with married men since my divorce. Neither of them worked out."

"Why not?"

"Oh, generally because it was their wives who really understood them and me who didn't - until I'd spent several months believing them when they said were serious about changing their lives." She paused. "They were looking for excitement really, like little boys playing clandestine games. They just wanted some silly secrecy and romance in their lives."

"So, why did you see me again?"

"Because I liked you. And because you didn't plan what happened. And, I suppose, because you seemed so grateful for the attention - like a great big puppy that had just been given an affectionate stroke." She realised what she'd just said sounded patronising, " I'm sorry, that didn't come out as it was meant to. I just felt comfortable, that's all."

"Look down there," He pointed at the view through her window as they reached the top of the Downs. The countryside stretched out below them, green and yellow fields, and villages tucked in amongst the folds in the land, gathered around churches, their spires standing high above the surrounding trees. "I always feel exhilarated, when I come up here."

"It's great to feel free." She smiled. "It panders to our dreams. But you can't stay up here forever. At some point most of us are forced back into the real world. And then the small streets and cosy houses trap you inside. You tell yourself you want to escape but even when a door opens, most of us are afraid to go through unless we're forced to."

He could feel her mood had changed and waited for her to say more, but she stopped talking and sat silently alongside him.

"We'll be there shortly."

She nodded, pulled down the sun visor and checked her make-up in the mirror. "What will you do when we meet someone who knows Sally? It's bound to happen one day."

He should have known the answer; it was something he thought about every time they went out. "Sometimes I think it would be a relief. It would force everything to a conclusion. Other times I feel guilty, about how Sally would feel. She would see it as a betrayal, just another sign of my weakness."

"Do you ever feel guilty about me?" Sarah paused. "About the time I spend waiting to see you, or the hopes I might have?"

"What's brought this on?" He felt confused. "Five minutes ago, we were driving along happily, and now I feel I'm in the firing line. Look, I know it's difficult, but I was married when we started seeing each other."

"Forget it." She shook her head, "I just wonder sometimes who or what is more important to you - Sally and the shop or our relationship. If Sally found out about us, would you leave her or stop seeing me?"

" I'd leave if she found out. The guilt I'd feel is the main reason holding me back, so there'd be no point in staying afterwards. I'm not sure what would happen with the flat we live in, though, it goes with the store manager's job."

"You could move in with me and they might allow her to stay there – she works for the company as well."

"I'm not sure they would," he drove on, reached the pub, and turned into the car park. Now he felt he was failing Sarah like he'd failed Sally. Like he'd failed at work. The chronic sense of failure depressed him.

"Don't you want more out of life than opening and closing the store every day, and trying to please a wife who doesn't want to be there any more than you do?"

"I'm sorry," he looked down as he spoke, "I don't know what to say."

She could see he was upset and turned her face away, trying to hide the hurt she was feeling. "I'll be alright when I've had a drink. There's a space," she pointed to a spot beneath a large tree, "You can park there."

He parked, feeling the world below was like a rolling mist, following him onto the Downs and enveloping him - impairing his previously clear vision of what lay ahead. She pulled the sun visor down again and dabbed at her make-up with a tissue, before opening her door and getting out.

There were tables with parasols in front of the pub and the evening was still warm, so they chose to sit outside. He went into the bar, brought out their drinks and sat down next to her. As they talked, people continued arriving and the tables began to fill. He sat there, legs outstretched, and began to relax again as they talked. She leaned her head against the back of the seat.

"I didn't mean to go on at you. It's just that I've been on my own for so long. Even when I was married, I felt lonely. My husband used to hit the bottle - not like Jonah, but he had his moments. His friends used to think he was great, the life and soul of every lad's night out. They found it particularly amusing the night he crawled up the path on his hands and knees and threw-up in the flowerbed. They talked about it for weeks."

"I don't like getting drunk. I hate it when my head starts spinning. I felt dreadful the morning after we met."

"Well, you certainly know how to flatter a girl," she laughed. "I'd hoped I'd made a rather more favourable impression on you. Just for that, you can buy me another drink."

She finished her wine and placed the glass back on the table, stroking the long stem between her finger and thumb, reflectively, and then holding it out for him to take with him. "This girl's thirsty so I think I'd prefer a fruit juice rather than wine, please."

"Are you sure?"

"Absolutely, get me an orange juice, that will be good."

The way the evening had been going and the change in Sarah's choice of drinks was affecting Chris' confidence. Whatever else happened, he knew he didn't want to lose her and be left with Sally, the pair of them living miserably together in the flat above the store. He went inside and stood at the bar waiting to be served.

"Hi, Chris," a hand tapped him on the shoulder, "I didn't expect to see you here."

Chris recognised the voice, froze for a moment, then recovering himself, smiled and turned round. "I didn't expect to see you either, Jon, a bit away from where you usually drink isn't it."

"Yes, we decided to go for a drive, have a bit of a change. Linda's outside finding a seat. Are you sitting in here?" He looked round. "I didn't see Sally outside."

"Sally's not with me this evening," Chris put the glasses on the bar, "Look, I'll catch-up with you, I need to find the loo."

"OK, Linda will be pleased to see you, she's been saying for days that she needs to call Sally and arrange for us all to meet-up somewhere. What are you drinking? I'll get one in for you."

"No, thanks, I'm not sure whether I'm having another one, but I'll see you in a few minutes." He moved away in the general direction of the toilets and then detoured outside to try to collect Sarah without being seen. He found Linda sitting at the next table to Sarah and went back inside the bar. Jon had ordered his drinks and was carrying them out.

Chris wasn't sure what to do, but realised he couldn't avoid introducing Sarah, ordered their drinks and walked back out to face them. Jon and Linda both waved as he walked towards them, and Sarah smiled. "I thought I'd lost you," she said as she took the orange juice from him. "Are you, ok?"

"Fine, but I need to introduce you to some friends of mine," he turned to make the introduction. "Jon and Linda this is Sarah." There was a pause, everyone trying to evaluate the situation. "You're welcome to join us," Chris pointed to the spare seats at the table he and Sarah were sitting at.

Jon began to get up, but Linda placed her hand on his arm, pulled him back down and stayed seated.

"No, it's alright," Linda said, "We're not staying long. We can catch-up another time."

"No, please don't leave because of us, Chris was just saying he had to get home." Sarah drained her glass of juice. " Stay and enjoy yourselves." She smiled at a couple waiting to take their places, indicated they were leaving, then stood up and walked to the car. Chris took a quick mouthful of his lager, said goodbye to his friends and left the rest of his drink on the table.

"So, where do we go from here?" she asked as he drove away. "Do you think they'll tell Sally? How close are they?"

"Close. Linda and her have been friends for years."

"What if you have a chat to Jon? Maybe he can persuade her not to say anything."

"No, there's no way that's going to happen, and if Sally's going to find out about our relationship, she deserves to hear it from me."

"What will she do?"

"After she's finished blaming me for ruining her life?" He shrugged his shoulders. "I don't know. So, if you're still willing to have me at your place, I'll move in tomorrow."

"Are you sure about this? Linda might not say anything."

"I don't think that's likely; she'll enjoy telling Sally. And, anyway, Sally's bound to find out sooner or later. It was Jon and Linda tonight, another night it'll be someone else." He stopped outside her flat. "I'd better not come in; I need to talk to Sally before Linda calls. I'll call you tomorrow."

He got out, opened her door, and gave her a hug as she stood on the pavement.

"Speak to you tomorrow," she kissed him quickly, "And best of luck."

The flat was in darkness when he got back. He went into the kitchen and found a note propped up on the table: 'Andy called. Said it was important you 'phone him in the morning. Wouldn't leave a message. Going to bed.'

When he went to the bedroom, Sally was asleep. He got undressed and into bed without waking her and guessed she may have taken a pill, to help her sleep. He lay there thinking, unable to sleep himself for a while, realising it was the last night he'd spend with her. The next morning, Sally was still asleep when he woke. The thought of talking to her appalled him and he slipped out of bed and went to make himself a coffee. He picked Sally's note up again and decided to call Andy immediately, knowing he was always up early.

"Hi, Chris, bit early for you, isn't it? Anyway, I've got some great news. The Berwick Street store's come up again and we think you're just the man to run it."

"Are you calling Andy?" Sally walked into the kitchen, yawning, and interrupted the call.

He nodded and she turned away.

"I need to talk to you this morning, can you get across?" Andy asked, "We'd like to announce your appointment as soon as possible."

"Yes, I'll open up and meet you around 11.00, if that's ok?"

"Perfect, I'll see you then and we can firm up all the details. And congratulations, Chris, you've earned this."

"What's happened now?" Sally looked concerned, "You haven't done something stupid have you?"

"No, they're going to give me a bigger store."

"I've heard that one before. I'll believe it when I see it."

"It's definite. I'm going across to talk to Andy this morning."

"You mean we're really going to get out of this dingy little hole at last?" She sounded incredulous. "So, I can give up serving winos?"

"It's not quite as simple as that. We need to talk." He waited a moment to allow her to appreciate the importance of what he was about to say. "I know I told you I was at a Sales meeting yesterday evening, but I wasn't. I've been seeing somebody else, and we met Jon and Linda whilst we were out. I imagine Linda will be calling you shortly."

"What?" Sally stepped back, staring at him, finding it difficult to believe what he was telling her. "All these years I've had to put up with this dump and now, as soon as you get something better, you tell me you're leaving me. Don't be so stupid," she was almost sneering at him now, but he could see she was afraid, "She could drop you tomorrow. How long's it been going on?"

"For a few months now, ever since the annual convention. We met whilst I was in the bar with Andy afterwards."

Sally ignored what he was saying, "You're mad if you think I'm going to let you just walk away like this."

"I'm sorry, but you've got to let go, I'm leaving, whatever you say." He was amazed at the calmness in his voice, but physically he was shaking.

"What throw away everything I've stayed here for, just as things are looking up?"

"You've been making it clear our marriage has been dead for years. I thought you'd be pleased to get rid of me."

"What's she like?"

"You'll have to ask Linda," Chris avoided saying Sarah was younger and how he felt about her, realising the tirade of abuse it would bring down on him.

"How could you humiliate me like this, in front of our friends?"

"I'm sorry," he said it again. He was always saying 'sorry'. "I've got to open the store."

"Bugger the store", she tried to stop him going downstairs, but he managed to slide past her. "What about us and this new opportunity?"

"It's over, I'm sorry." He went down, opened the store and told the staff he was going out. As he left, he met Jonah lurching in. "Give him a couple of cans from me," he shouted to the girl at the till, and rushed away before Jonah could thank him.

As soon as he'd left, he called Sarah. Her reaction wasn't what he'd anticipated.

"We need to talk. Can you meet me for lunch after you've spoken to Andy? It's important."

"You're not backing out now, are you?" He panicked.

"No, of course not. But we need to talk."

He met her in the park and sat down next to her on their usual bench.

"This hasn't worked out in the way I wanted," she hesitated, seeming nervous. "I wanted you to choose me, now I'll never know if you did or whether events just overtook us. If we hadn't met your friends last night, you'd still be with Sally, and, how would I have fitted into your new plans then?"

"This isn't something I've ever done before." He turned and faced her. "You know you're important to me. I would have left her eventually, when I came to terms with my guilt."

"It's easy for you to say that now. But how will I ever be sure you wouldn't have let things just drift on?" She kept watching his face, waiting for his answer.

"You were like this last night, and I don't understand why it has suddenly become such an issue." Chris felt apprehensive. "Things are different now and I understand it must be scary for you. If you want time to think about it, or even back out - it's got to be your decision. But I do want you and I'm not going back to Sally."

"It's not that simple. Supposing you'd had children with Sally. How would you have handled things then?"

"It may have been different, harder," he paused to think. "I guess she may have been happier and blamed me less for everything. But that's not what happened, and it doesn't make any sense to ask yourself questions about what might have been."

"Why didn't you have children?"

"I don't know. We tried, but I guess I just failed again. At least that's the way Sally sees it."

"What about having children with me?"

"I'd like to, assuming I can, if that's what you want. But shouldn't we take one step at a time? Perhaps spend more time getting to know each other better?"

"We don't have that luxury." She looked at him intently. "I think I'm pregnant, that's why I was pushing so hard to find out how you felt last night."

Chris was stunned, staring at her as he took in what she'd told him. "Are you sure?"

"The test was positive, but I only took it a couple of days back. I've still got to make an appointment with my doctor."

"I can't believe it. That's fantastic." Chris was ecstatic. "I always wanted kids, but I'd grown to believe it was me that couldn't have them. She never said it might be her."

"That's the problem with you, you always assume it's your fault."

"Why didn't you tell me last night?"

"Because I wanted you to choose me, rather than feel you had to leave her." She looked at him again. "Now, I'll never be certain what you'd have decided."

He stood up, took her arm and lifted her up from the bench. "I guess I'll just have to show you." He put his arm around her, gave her a quick hug, and started walking with her round the park, a contented smile on his face.

Walking under a ladder

Most passers-by looked ahead as they walked along the pavement. They saw the ladder, placed against the scaffolding, and walked around it, either from superstition or fear that something might fall on them whilst the men were working above. But not everyone walked around and, as Jonah approached, one of the builders looked down, nudged his mate and pointed at the ragged figure on the pavement.

"Hey, take a look at this guy, I'll put money on him walking under the bloody ladder."

They watched as the figure in the charcoal-coloured overcoat struggled along, a red vinyl shopping bag hanging from his hand, muttering to himself and oblivious to what was ahead of him.

"Told you," the builder nodded to his mate as the figure walked on without looking up, "Out of his head already." He shouted down, "Oi, that's bloody bad luck, mate, walking under a ladder."

But Jonah's mind was busy, and he didn't hear the shouted warning.

"Not sure the poor bastard's had much luck in his life, anyway," the second builder turned back to what he'd been doing, "So I don't reckon walking under a ladder's going to make much difference."

Jonah walked on, still unaware of having invited any impending bad luck. The thing that was concentrating his mind was the hole in one of his shoes and the discomfort it was causing him. He needed some new shoes urgently. The old pair had lasted well, been good friends over the past year or so and Jonah would be sad to see them go – they'd been comfortable, but their days were over.

Fortunately, the weather had been dry for the past few days and he'd been able to walk around whilst he searched for a new pair, without his feet getting wet. But, despite his efforts, he hadn't found any. He'd tried to look through some bags left outside a charity shop but been waved away by one of the volunteers as the shop was opening. And the volunteers at the hostel hadn't got any his size. So now he was on his way to the Salvation Army, hoping they might have a pair that fitted him. The Army was on the other side of the city centre and, as he hobbled there, he cursed his shoes for causing him so much discomfort.

It wasn't only the distance that concerned Jonah, it was also the way the weather was changing; the sky had clouded over, and it felt as though it was going to rain. Jonah tried to walk faster, but couldn't, the cans in his shopping bag weighing him down. He decided to cut through the park and stop for a drink, satisfying his thirst and making the bag lighter at the same time. There was an old shelter about halfway through, brick built with a long wooden bench along the back wall. The rain was starting as he reached it, and he sat down on the bench, relieved to be in the dry.

He took a can out of his bag, pulled back the tab and prepared to sit out the downpour. As he tossed his head back and started to drink, he caught a sudden movement and flinched instinctively, anticipating danger. The person running into the shelter reacted similarly, not expecting anyone to be there. Jonah took a quick glance at the newcomer and then looked away again. He was a young lad in his teens and Jonah was immediately apprehensive and moved further into the nearest corner. The boy ignored Jonah and sat in the opposite corner from him, hands in his pockets, and hood down over his bowed head.

Jonah took another mouthful of lager, then stole another look at the boy. The boy didn't move, not appearing to notice, locking himself inside his hood. "You alright?" Jonah muttered, trying to assess the boy's mood and whether he was likely to be attacked. But the boy stayed staring at his feet. Jonah shrugged and continued drinking. Halfway down the can, Jonah fancied a smoke, found a roll-up in his pocket and lit it. The boy coughed, his hands still in his pockets. "Fag botherin' yer?" Jonah asked. This time the boy shook his head, indicating he was alright with the smoke, but it wasn't a convincing gesture.

The two of them continued sitting in the shelter ignoring each other. Jonah watched the rain falling and thought about his leaking shoe and the walk to the Salvation Army. He felt less afraid of the boy who still hadn't spoken and whose head remained covered by his hood. "Aint got a few coppers you can spare, 'ave you?" he asked the young guy. The lad shook his head without looking up; "Only ah need some shoes," Jonah pointed at the rain outside, "Me shoes leak, get me feet wet." This time the lad took a quick look across at Jonah's feet, but then turned away again without saying anything.

The rain continued and Jonah heard voices and footsteps running towards the shelter. A new face appeared round the wall, a lad with short, dark hair. "Christ, look who we've got here, it's bloody Psycho." He pointed at the boy in the corner as a second lad joined him. "And he's found a friend at last, Psycho's found a bloody wino as a friend.

"About the only fucking person who would be friends with him," the second lad stood there smirking, "Filthy old bastard, too. So, Psycho, tell your friend to give us one of his bloody cans."

The hooded boy in the corner didn't react.

"Well, if you're not going to ask your mate to give us a drink, we'll have to help ourselves." He turned to his mate, "I fancy a drink, don't you?"

"Yeah," the dark-haired lad stepped forward and reached out to take Jonah's bag.

Jonah snatched the bag from the floor and held it firmly against his chest, refusing to let it go. He sat still, staring at the lad, defiant but afraid.

"Give us your bag old man or you'll get what's coming to you." The lad took another step towards Jonah who froze, trapped against the walls of the shelter.

"Leave him alone," the boy in the corner jumped up and stood in front of Jonah, shielding him, "That bag's all he's got in the world, even his shoes are leaking. Why don't you go and pick on someone else?"

"My God, Psycho's got a voice," the lad turned to his mate, then turned back, "For the same reason we pick on you, Psycho, because he's a fucking outcast."

The boy with the hood said nothing, but stayed where he was in front of Jonah, not willing to see the old man humiliated any further. The other lad stiffened and faced-up to him.

"Come on, he's not worth bothering with," the second lad pulled his mate's arm, urging him to back-off, "We can deal with Psycho some other time. Leave him with his manky friend."

Outside the shelter, the rain had stopped, and the two lads began to move away, the dark-haired one turning back and spitting on the ground, before walking-off, laughing with his mate.

"Thanks," Jonah muttered as the lad with the hood turned round to check he was alright, "I owes yer."

The lad shook his head and smiled briefly, denying any reason for gratitude. The path and grass were wet after the rain, but Jonah had to get to the Salvation Army centre and find some shoes. He stood up, ready to leave but the lad who'd protected him held up his hand and motioned him to stay where he was.

"What size shoe do you wear?" he asked, surprising Jonah who'd got used to him not speaking.

Jonah shook his head, not sure what size he was wearing. "Dunno, 'aven't looked."

The lad sat down next to him and placed one of his shoes alongside Jonah's, comparing the lengths. "It looks like you're an eight," he looked at Jonah to see if he'd prompted any recollection about his shoe size, "I'm a nine and my shoe is longer."

"'Bout right, I think," Jonah muttered, 'Why? You ain't gonna give me your shoes are yer?" He looked covetously at the shoes the lad was wearing.

"No way," the lad laughed, "These are really expensive trainers," he named a brand, but Jonah didn't recognise it, "But my Mum's got some shoes she's been waiting to take to a charity shop and they're a size eight."

"I ain't wearing women's shoes," Jonah shook his head stubbornly.

"They're men's shoes," the lad smiled for the first time and stood up, "And our house is nearby, we can walk there in a few minutes."

Jonah hesitated, unsure what to do; whether to go to the Salvation Army as he'd planned, or to go with the lad, not knowing where he was being taken.

"Come on, there's nothing to worry about," the lad stepped out of the shelter and turned round, beckoning Jonah to follow him. "My mum and sister are at home."

The thought of the new shoes and the way the lad had defended him made up Jonah's mind; he grabbed his bag and followed him out. They walked together through the park and then turned into some residential streets near the university buildings. The lad had stopped talking again and they walked in silence, Jonah concentrating on the moisture leaking through the hole in his shoe and not noticing the comparative quietness of the tree-lined streets or the older style houses that lined them.

A small girl was playing on a scooter in the drive of one of the houses and, when she saw Jonah and the lad approaching, she ran towards the house and called to her mother. "Mummy, Paul's coming home, and he's got someone with him." A woman emerged and the small girl pointed down the street towards her brother who was walking home with what appeared to be a tramp.

"Who's that man Paul's with?" the little girl asked, "He looks very dirty."

Her mother shook her head, "I really don't know, Becky." She waved to her son and thought again how tall he was getting, comparing him with the smaller, slightly bent man beside him, dressed in a scruffy coat and carrying a red shopping bag. It had been difficult bringing Paul up, he was reclusive, and she'd been praying for ages he would find himself a friend, someone he could feel comfortable talking to; but the tramp didn't fit any of the mental images she'd played with. She looked quizzically at him as she stood aside and let them both through the gate.

Paul turned to her to explain what was happening. "Hi, Mum, I've bought this guy back because he needs some new shoes. I reckon he's about size eight, the same as those old shoes of grandad's, the ones you were going to take to the charity shop."

His mother looked down at Jonah's feet and nodded, "Looks around the same size. Becky, can you show this gentleman round to the conservatory," she pointed to the rear of the house, "He can try the shoes on there, I'll be with you in a minute." The girl got back on her scooter and waved at Jonah to follow her.

His mother put her hand on Paul's shoulder, restraining him for a moment, "Where did you find him?" she mouthed silently.

"In the shelter in the park, it was raining, and we were both trying to keep dry. And then a couple of the guys from school came along, started to take the piss out of me and then tried to steal some of his drink." Paul pointed at Jonah's bag. "Sorry, but I don't know his name."

His mother nodded and she and Paul followed Becky and Jonah down the path towards a tall timber gate. Paul opened the gate, then opened the conservatory door for Jonah and pointed at a chair, indicating he should sit in it. The furniture inside was made from bamboo, low, with cushions faded by the sun and Jonah found it difficult to get seated. When he was settled, Paul's mother asked him his name.

"Jonah." The answer was short.

"I'm Ellen, and Paul's my son. And, as you've probably gathered, this is Becky," she pointed at her daughter, smiling as she tried to put Jonah at ease. "So, Jonah, would you like a cup of tea or something to eat?" Jonah shook his head and she turned back to her son. "Ok, Paul, so what made you become involved in this?" She looked for any sign of him being in a fight but couldn't see anything.

Paul thought for a while, trying to sort his thoughts out, then lowered his voice before answering. "His drink was all he had, Mum, you should have seen his face when they tried to take it, he looked so scared and helpless. And he didn't know how to deal with them – it was like I feel when I have to talk to people. But this time it wasn't me who was stressed and, somehow, that made it easier, I didn't have to interact with them, just stop what they were doing to him."

"So, how did they react, when you stood up to them?"

"They backed-off, that was the strange thing, I thought they might start bullying me, but they didn't."

"Right," Ellen looked down at Jonah, "You sit here, and I'll go and look out those shoes." When she returned, she was carrying a pair of shoes, and a large plastic bag. "Here we are," she put the shoes down in front of Jonah, "Take those shoes off and try these, they look as though they'll fit you."

Jonah took off his own shoes, displaying his wet socks as he reached for the polished brown replacements.

"Wait, you need to take those socks off, they're soaking." Ellen held out a hand to restrain Jonah, sent Becky to find a towel and asked Paul to fetch a pair of dry socks from upstairs. Jonah dried his feet, put on the socks and then the shoes, tightening the laces as soon as they felt comfortable. He pushed himself up from the low chair he'd been sitting in and tried walking a couple of paces.

"How do they feel?" Ellen asked.

Jonah nodded; "Good," he looked at the shoes, new and shiny on his feet, "Feel good."

Ellen opened the plastic bag, took out a jumper and a shirt and motioned Jonah to stand in front of her,

"Now, while you're here, let's see if we can give you a new wardrobe as well." Jonah stood where she'd indicated, his head bent whilst she held both garments up to make sure they'd fit. Satisfied, she folded them and then held a pair of trousers against his legs. They seemed the right size and length, and she put those back in the bag with the shirt and pullover and added an old leather belt she'd found.

Jonah took his new, neatly folded clothes, picked-up his bag of booze and raised his finger to his forehead, nodding and thanking her.

"Don't go yet," Ellen disappeared indoors and re-emerged with her bag. She took some money out of her purse and gave it to him, "Here, take this and try not to spend it on booze."

'Thank 'ee," Jonah turned to leave. "And thank 'ee too," he looked-up at Paul and nodded.

"You'd better walk him back to the park, Paul, in case he doesn't remember the way."

Paul nodded and escorted Jonah outside. As they were leaving, Ellen smiled down at Becky, "At least my dad's old clothes will do someone some good, I reckon he might be quite amused if he could see old Jonah, walking around in them. Good job they were a similar size."

"But grandad didn't smell like that man does," Becky looked-up at her mother, "He stinks."

"Ssh," Ellen raised her finger to her lips, "He might be upset if he hears you say something like that. "Come on, we'd better see them off."

When they were outside, she called her son to stop for a moment. "You've done a really good thing today, I'm proud of you - for being kind, as well as standing-up to those other lads. Go on," she pointed at Jonah, "Take him back to where you found him."

Paul smiled, turned back to catch-up with Jonah, and walked silently on to the entrance to the park. This time he didn't pull his hood over his head as they walked along together. "Bye," was all he said as he turned to leave.

"Thank 'ee," Jonah was no more generous with his own goodbye, turned and began walking towards the opposite park entrance and back into the city centre. As he approached the street where he'd walked beneath the ladder earlier in the day, he looked down again at his bright new shoes. There were flagstones beneath the shoes, and he realised he was standing on a line. Recalling it was unlucky to tread on the lines, he concentrated on placing his feet in the squares and was still looking down as he approached the scaffolding the builders were working on.

"Here comes that bloody wino again," the builder turned to his mate, "Let's see what he does this time." They both watched as Jonah passed under the ladder, concentrating on where he was placing his feet. "Some blokes never learn, do they?" the builder shook his head, "Poor old sod."

When he got to the end of the flagstones and back onto some asphalt paving, Jonah relaxed and started to walk normally again, murmuring to himself something about having better luck. A man was approaching, and he held out his hand expectantly, and asked for money to buy some food. The man avoided him and continued walking.

Jonah's Pink Period

Jonah felt tired as he walked towards the town centre. The day was warm, and his sleep had been disturbed when Mac got out of his hostel bed and begun shouting during the night. And then other people had started shouting and remonstrating, the lights had gone on and, in the chaos that followed, Mac had been escorted out by the hostel staff. Jonah had tried to go back to sleep, but once awake it had been difficult and he'd lain there a while restless and wanting a drink. Then he'd been woken at the usual time for breakfast, before collecting his bag with his booze and leaving the hostel.

His original intention had been to walk into town immediately but, as he reached the bridge across the river, he looked down and spotted an empty seat. The warmth of the morning and his tiredness urged him down the steps and onto the bank, and he told himself there would still be a chance of cadging some money in town later. Arriving at the bench, he sat down, reached into his bag and took out one of the cans of extra strong lager. He drank it hungrily and then opened a second. The second can compounded his tiredness, and he took off his coat, folded it into a pillow, placed his bag behind him and fell asleep.

Oblivious to the world around him, he didn't notice the two young boys standing on the bridge and pointing down at him, or the way they grinned and nodded to each other. And he wasn't aware of them walking down the steps and taking a can of hair colouring out of a bag that one of them was carrying. They approached carefully, concerned about waking him, shook the can and then sprayed the colouring onto his hair. Satisfied with the effect, they walked back to the bridge and continued their journey. The colouring dried as Jonah slept and when he awoke and set off into town, he was unaware of the change in his appearance.

However, as he approached the shopping precinct, he realised people were looking at him, nudging each other and pointing. And those that did give him money were grinning, amused instead of appearing concerned as they usually did. Then people began taking photos of him, holding-up their 'phones and sharing the images. At first, he felt irritated, but then his mood changed as more people began to give him money. He smiled and started playing-up to the photographers, anxious to increase the flow of funds, but still unaware of what was creating the changed reactions around him.

......

Iain was in the local newspaper's office when the calls about the wino and photos of Jonah began to come through. Jonah and Iain had met before but, on those occasions, Jonah had not been resplendent with startling pink hair. By the time Iain arrived at the precinct, the local television reporter was also there, interviewing shoppers who were amused by Jonah's antics: a short jig, followed by some theatrical bows and a walk round the crowd with an outstretched hand and happy nods of appreciation when anyone gave him money. Then another jig as more shoppers stopped to watch. The reporter tried to engage Jonah but with only her microphone to catch his attention failed to get anything other than his name and retreated. Iain took some photos and waited for the crowd to move on before trying his own approach, a packet of cigarettes held out to attract Jonah's interest.

'Don't mind if ah do," Jonah attempted to take the packet, but Iain pulled it away, took out two of the cigarettes and gave them to him.

"You can have the rest, after you've spoken to me," Iain put the packet back in his pocket, produced a box of matches and lit the cigarette. Jonah inhaled deeply and Iain waited before speaking, unsure whether the deep breath was intended to ensure the cigarette was lit or a reaction to the unusual energy Jonah had expended during his jigs. "So why did you dye your hair?" he asked when he decided Jonah was ready to talk.

Jonah looked confused, "What about me 'air?"

"It's bright pink," Iain grinned, "Why do you think all those shoppers were taking photos? Come over here and take a look at yourself in the mirror." He motioned Jonah across to a shop with a large mirror in the window.

Jonah's face was a mixture of wonder and anger. "'Ow did that 'appen? 'Oo did this to me? They ain't got no right. Nobody's got any right." He ran his dirty fingers through his hair, then rubbed it to get the colour off.

"Hey, don't get so upset, think of it like being painted by Picasso – he had a pink period. Look on this as your pink period." Iain was finding it difficult not to laugh.

"It ain't funny," Jonah was not amused, "And 'oo the 'ell was this bloody Piccasi bloke? 'Oo painted 'im?"

"Picasso, you must have heard of him, the famous artist." Iain shook his head, "Nobody painted him, he used to paint other people. Spanish guy."

"They bloody painted me. 'Ow'm ah gonna get it off?" Jonah was beginning to appear distressed, "Look bloody silly like this."

"You'll need a shower to get that off."

"Where'm ah gonna get a shower? Don't want a bloody shower." Jonah was shaking his head, looking abjectly at his reflection.

Iain began to feel sorry for Jonah and thought for a moment. He'd been researching the issues of homelessness and addiction for some time and Jonah's temporary transformation gave him a powerful opportunity to talk about them. "I think I can help you there," Iain pulled his 'phone out of his pocket, "And there may be some money for booze too." He dialled a number and called a hairdresser he knew. "Yes, he's likely to be on local tv tonight, the reporter was here, and we can run an article online and in tomorrow's paper – you know, sympathetic hair stylist, before and after photo, the attitudes towards homeless people and the issues they face. It'll give you some free coverage." He listened to the response and then turned to Jonah, "Look, I know this hairdresser who will get rid of the dye for you, and I'll give you the rest of the packet of fags and some money for booze. How's that sound?"

"'Ow much?" Jonah held out his hand.

"That depends on whether you play ball," Iain shook his head, "You can have the fags now, but you'll have to wait for the money."

Jonah started muttering and Iain began to withdraw the cigarette packet, "Alright," Jonah nodded his head and grabbed the cigarettes as Iain held them out again.

"Right, we need to walk a couple of streets away," Iain pointed in the direction of the hairdressers. Jonah picked up his bag and shambled along beside him, his pink hair still attracting glances from passers-by. When they reached the salon, Iain opened the door and ushered Jonah in. "Hi,

Kieran, this is the guy I was telling you about. I'm afraid he's going to need a lot of attention; don't suppose he's washed his hair in weeks. "

"I can see why he attracted so much attention," the other man walked round Jonah looking at his hair but was frustrated when Jonah spun round, suspicious of what was going on. "It's not exactly a subtle pink, is it?"

"Shouldn't be bloody pink at all," Jonah grumbled, "Don't know 'ow it got pink, wasn't pink this mornin' at the 'ostel."

"Misha will soon have it back to its usual colour, won't you Misha?" Kieran called across to one of the girls in the salon. He pointed at Jonah's thickly matted hair and winked discreetly, "And I think you'll need to wear some disposable gloves and sterilise the comb afterwards, Misha."

"Let me take your bag and coat," Misha stepped forward her hands held out, but Jonah backed away, "It's alright they'll be safe, I'll put them in the cupboard."

Jonah looked at Iain for reassurance and, when he nodded, reluctantly let go of his bag and undid the coarse piece of string that kept his coat wrapped round him. He watched as Misha opened the cupboard and placed both at one end, separating them as far as possible from the other items hanging there.

"I guess we ought to have a 'before' photo," Iain motioned Jonah to stand still and took his 'phone out of his pocket.

"Don't want me photo taken," Jonah looked defiantly across, but gave way when Iain threatened to take him back out again and leave him pink-haired on the street. Instead, he stood sour faced as Iain took a couple of shots, before being led away to the basin to have his hair untangled and washed.

Iain looked at the photo and showed it to Kieran, "Miserable old bugger - should make the 'after' photo look even better!"

Their conversation was interrupted by more complaints from Jonah as Misha lowered the back of his chair and placed his head against the basin. The complaints increased as she started to wet his hair with the shower head and got even louder when she started to run the comb through the mess of knots, pulling the skin on his scalp as his hair resisted.

"Sorry, but your hair is very tangled," Misha was finding it difficult to keep a straight face and, as Jonah's cries grew more frequent, started giggling. Jonah tried to sit up, but she placed her hand on his shoulder and told him to keep his eyes closed in case the shampoo irritated them. She began to rinse the first shampoo off and, when she'd finished, Jonah tried to get up again. She pushed him back down and began to apply a second round of shampoo.

"'Ere, what you doing?" Jonah was shaking his head, but she held it firmly in place whilst she massaged the shampoo into his hair, "You've already done me 'air."

"Sorry, Jonah," Kieran grabbed a glove, walked across and placed a restraining hand on his arm, "You've still got the conditioner to come."

"Don't want to be conditioned, don't need conditioning," Jonah protested.

"I'm afraid you do," Kieran's voice became more insistent, "We've never had a head of hair so tangled and knotted. You really should try to look after your hair better. And when Misha's finished with you, we'll give you a cut –

it doesn't look as though it's been cut properly for years."

"Don't want it cut."

"Well, I'm sorry but we couldn't possibly let you leave without tidying it up, it would be bad for our salon's reputation." Kieran tutted and shook his head, "What do you think people would think of us if they saw you walking out with your hair as it is?"

Jonah began to protest again but, as soon as she had washed the shampoo away for the second time, Misha applied the conditioner without giving Jonah time to struggle up. Finally, she got a towel and began to dry Jonah's hair, then took him across to one of the stylists' chairs to show him the pink dye had gone.

"So, how would you like your hair cut and styled?" Kieran asked.

"Dunno, don't want it cut," Jonah protested, "People'll take the piss."

"They won't take the piss any more than they did when it was bright pink," Iain intervened, "Just cut it how you think it should be cut, Kieran. And when you're finished, give him a shave, make him look his best for the 'after' photo."

"Ah can shave meself," Jonah muttered.

"If you don't have a shave, you'll have to find your own money to buy your booze," Iain shook his head. "We need you to look good when you leave here, not untidy and stubbly like you are now. Besides, it'll save you the bother of shaving for a few days. So, what's it going to be, a shave and money for booze or nothing."

Jonah said nothing. Just sat scowling in his chair.

"I'll take that as a 'yes' to a shave," Iain nodded to Kieran to continue, and Jonah raised no more vocal objections but remained scowling. When Kieran finished his hair Jonah looked very different from when he'd come in. "That's fantastic," Iain shook his head in disbelief, "I've never seen Jonah look like he does now."

"Won't see me bloody look like it again," Jonah examined his reflection in the mirror and Kieran smiled as he saw a quick look of surprise and pride.

"Right, let's get started on the shave," Kieran tilted the chair gently backwards, "Just relax, Jonah, enjoy being pampered, other people pay a lot of money for this experience." He tucked a towel around Jonah's neck and then placed a warm flannel around his face. Jonah attempted one last protest, but realised it was futile and lay back. Kieran prepared the shaving cream, removed the flannel and began to brush the lather onto Jonah's face. When he'd finished, he picked up his razor and opened the blade. The sight of the open razor made Jonah flinch and Kieran had to warn him to keep still. When he was satisfied that Jonah's skin was smooth and clear of bristles, Kieran washed his face, placed a final warm towel across it and removed any remaining streaks of lather.

Once Jonah was sat up again, Iain took a couple of photos and shared them with Kieran, whilst Misha fetched Jonah's coat and bag from the cupboard.

"Do you want to see the photos, Jonah?" Iain held the shots out for Jonah to look at.

"Just want me money," Jonah ignored the photos, held his hand out and took the notes Iain gave him. "That all?" he frowned, "Don't seem much."

"It'll pay for the hostel tonight and buy you some booze," Iain shook his head, "I'm sorry Jonah, there isn't any more to give you."

As Jonah walked off down the street, he noticed people looking at him. A woman approached, shook her head sympathetically and pressed some money into his hand. A man took out his wallet and murmured something about 'falling on hard times'. By the time Jonah was back in the City Centre he had collected more than enough money for a second night in the hostel.

"Bloody 'ell, what they done to yer, Jonah?" Mac was surprised at the transformation in Jonah's appearance when they met up on the way back to the hostel. " 'Eard you'd dyed yer 'air pink, now yer skin's all pink, just like a baby's bum. And yer 'air's all fluffed up. Yer look, like a bloody tart."

"Didn't dye me 'air, sommun' must've done it when ah was asleep," Jonah elbowed Mac away. "It were me pink period, like that famous artist bloke, Picassi – 'e 'ad one too."

"So, 'ow come yer 'air's not pink now?" Mac asked. "'Ow did yer get it off?"

"Went to this 'airdresser. Got 'im to do me 'air an' give me a shave."

"'Ow did yer pay for that?" Mac was confused, sure that Jonah couldn't have afforded to pay himself.

"Got friends, ain't I," Jonah was beginning to enjoy taunting Mac, "More'n you 'ave."

Mac swore and pushed through the hostel door. Jonah followed and handed his booze in at reception, then checked his money was still there and thrust it deeper into his trouser pocket, afraid of being robbed during the night.

......

Iain worked half the night on his article, and it appeared online and in the late edition of the paper the next day. It featured photos of Jonah dancing, pink-haired, in the town centre and talked about the abuse the homeless, like Jonah, experienced, and the negative emotions they encountered. He had no idea how Jonah had ended up living between the hostel and the street and found it difficult to imagine the hardness of his existence, sharing the apartness people felt when they passed Jonah in his scruffy old coat and his bag with his booze. And there was an 'after' photo showing the difference an hour of professional hairstyling and a shave could achieve and asking readers whether the manicured image of Jonah changed their beliefs about the inevitability of people like him remaining homeless?

The article ended with Iain taking a wider view; middle aged guys like Jonah were the obvious examples of homelessness, but there were hidden examples too: younger people who had left home and were sofa-surfing, abused women in temporary safe places. Jonah was just the visible tip of a larger social iceberg. Seizing on the article and wanting to join in the discussion, the local tv also ran a piece in its early evening news programmes, introducing it with the original video of Jonah and his pink hair.

When Jonah got back to the hostel, one of the staff gave him a copy of the local paper and congratulated him on becoming a celebrity and helping shed light on homelessness. Jonah took the paper and put it in his bag. He ate alone that evening, avoiding the smirks and comments of Mac and the others about his haircut, shave and new-found celebrity. The following morning, he made straight for the town centre, holding the article with his photos in one hand and using the other to ask for money. People pointed and took shots with their phones again, and a few asked to pose with him. Jonah had never received as much money before and encouraged, went back to the town centre the following few days.

But, as the news coverage faded, so did Jonah's new look. His hair became greasy and matted again, and his stubble reappeared. And the more he became like his old self, the less attention he attracted, although Mac and the others stopped taunting him. Most worrying for Jonah, however, was the reduction in the money he received. So, he decided to re-trace his steps, back to the hair salon.

As the door opened Kieran turned round and was horrified when Jonah walked in. "What are you doing here?"

"Need me 'air washed," Jonah pointed at his head.

"I'm sorry that's not possible," Kieran shook his head in denial, "Our other customers would stop coming if they saw you here. What we did was a one-off, we weren't busy, and it offered us a free opportunity of promoting our services, but we've been there and done that now."

"What abaht a shave?" Jonah felt his chin, the stubble rough against his fingers.

"No way," Kieran shook his head violently, "You couldn't afford one."

Misha finished washing a client's hair, led them across to Kieran's chair and made sure they were comfortable. "Kieran," she pulled him aside, "Look, it's quiet and we've got nothing on for the next half hour, and your client who's waiting is happy for Jonah to have a wash – I think he's pretty amused by the whole situation. So, can I give Jonah one last wash? Please. I feel sorry for the old boy." She put on the most appealing face she could. "Nobody's going to notice Jonah, the basins are at the back of the shop."

Kieran hesitated then gave in and nodded. He waved a finger at Jonah before Misha took his coat and bag, "This is the last time, understand?"

"Thank 'ee, Sir" Jonah raised a finger to his forehead in acknowledgement, "And seeing 'ow it 'elps promote your establishment 'ere, maybe you could spare a few pence for somethin' to eat, ah aven't eaten all day." He held out his hand, but Misha saw Kieran's face change colour and ushered him hurriedly away.

Cardboard Christmas

He lay in the black hole,
With its concrete ramps and pathways.
People passed through in the morning
On their way to somewhere,
Hurrying to offices, shops,
Places they belonged.
Then hurrying back in the evenings
To somewhere warm,
With soft settees
And feather duvets.
People still above the horizon,
Still defying gravity.

He lay cold, alone,
His coat tied tightly round him.
Wrapped in a blanket
Like a Christmas turkey,
And squeezed into a cardboard box
To keep out the wind.

He'd been sucked down slowly,
Then slower,
Hovering, for what seemed like an eternity
To those still interested enough to watch.
But to him it had happened suddenly,
His world imploding
As he disappeared into the dark.

Today, there were no people
Struggling with large bags
On their way back home.
No shops with windows bright
In the early evening darkness.
No light reflecting from
Glittering glass balls
And shimmering
On the artificial snow below.
No trains, no passing cars, no noise.
No presents, hopes, no childlike joys.
No Santa Claus.

Jonah's Reverie
(included as a chapter in 'No Smoke without Fire')

It had been a warm September. Jonah lay beneath a willow on the riverbank, his charcoal-coloured overcoat folded into a pillow and the sleeves of his red-check shirt rolled up. He was drinking strong lager and there were two or three empty cans thrown down by his feet.

Initially, the drink had relaxed him. But as he drank more, he began to feel an increasingly pervasive panic that displaced any other mental pictures he tried to view. His innate dread of the winter ahead blanketed his mind, destroying his casual enjoyment of the warmth and stillness of the afternoon.

He wished the winter were behind him and with it the dark, cold days filled with depression and fit only to sleep through. Winter was a time of survival until the next summer when, God willing, he would still be alive. Some friends would be gone, their places in the hostel queues taken by newer, younger bodies who pushed and shoved more vigorously.

Jonah smelt the air, anxious to enjoy it to the full. It was subtly scented after the gross summer perfumes, and delicately dry now that the oppressive humidity had gone. But he could not enjoy it for long, the winter haunted him. The warm afternoon and gentle ampleness of the grassy bank no longer existed. He looked inwardly and felt the loneliness welling up from his stomach, until it reached his throat and forced tears from his eyes by the strength of its pressure.

Even if there had been someone to put their arms around him, it was not enough. It would be a temporary comfort but not a timely one. His distress was from another time. Inside him there was a memory that kept breaking into his present, a memory from which he might temporarily distract himself but to which he continually returned.

The fourth can was empty, and his head was beginning to spin. He heard the voice of the woman he had known and concentrated upon her. She emerged from out of the darkness; onto the stage his mind was creating. He felt her touch him, her body softly close upon his.

"I was bloody in love with you", he mumbled.

"No, you just needed me." Her voice was soft, reminiscing.

"But you didn't bloody love me ", he accused.

"Perhaps", she turned her head away.

"You didn't. Look at me." His fingers gently turned her cheek. "I knew you didn't. That time we were in bed together."

"No, I was not in love with you. But I wanted you to be satisfied and, if you had asked me to, I would have stayed with you."

"But you left me." He lay across the old sofa and watched her walk away. She passed into the hall, and he heard the front door of the flat close behind her. "I didn't feel alone when we were together," he called after the image.

"You were always alone, particularly when you'd been drinking. The words would come tumbling out, sodden with resentment or self-pity. But I still didn't know whether it was the real you. And anyway, you weren't in love with me."

Her voice was firm, and he could not break through the barrier and touch her.

"If I had been I would have felt more vulnerable, more alone. I wasn't in love, but I was contented - and I wasn't afraid."

"That was only because you were younger." She swept her brown hair from her face. "You would have been afraid eventually. There was nothing that could distract you from yourself. Nothing that could keep you from looking inwards."

"I wanted to satisfy you, to make you love me." The tears rolled down Jonah's cheeks and he shuddered.

"It sounds as though it was yourself you were satisfying." Her voice was crisper.

"I was lonely. All I wanted was some company, somebody who would cuddle me as I fell asleep and who I could wake in the night without angering."

"I wasn't angry." Her voice softened.

"Did you have me just because I wanted you?" He asked.

"No, because I wanted to. Because you were close and warm. And because I had my own reasons for wanting someone."

"Why did you go?"

"Ssh", she put her finger against his lips, and he could smell the light sweetness of her perfume. "Don't, it was a different time."

"It was a golden generation I saw it in the papers. They wrote about it all the time. We asked questions."

"But they weren't new questions." She was always so sensible. "And we didn't find any new answers. Everybody rushed around, inventing new dances, wearing new fashions, persuading themselves that they were doing something that previous generations hadn't. Everybody but you."

"What did I do wrong?" He asked.

"You didn't do anything wrong. You turned against the flamboyance and tried to douse it with the cynical flood that burst through the walls which you erected against the world." She shook her head sadly.

"I didn't build any walls they were there already."

"Only because you couldn't stop questioning your existence. You couldn't forget your logic and join in the irrational fun." Now she sounded bitter as though their meetings had deprived her of something irreplaceable. "I needed to go out, to dance and scream at the music, but you wouldn't let me. You couldn't stand in a crowd without contempt for its enjoyment. To you it was all hollow."

"I enjoyed our evenings together. The music and the clothes, they were just drugs, things that made you feel high. But it was all meaningless."

"But nobody wanted to hear about that. They wanted to be happy."

"They were fools."

"No more foolish than you." Her voice was cold. "You found your own drug to hide behind. It made you feel good for a while. And sometimes, when it depressed you, you would drink more until you fell asleep. It was the sleep you really wanted, an anaesthetic to protect your sensitive soul."

"You didn't even like me."

"Oh yes, I liked you. And I would have stayed with you. Your vulnerability was attractive. But each time I came back you put your arm around me and submerged yourself in a temporary comfort which ignores passing seasons and pretends that, finally, we won't be alone."

She ran her finger against his cheek and his reverie was broken as he felt it catch against the unshaven bristles.

"Then why did you leave me?"

He felt cold as the afternoon began to merge with the evening and he recalled the cosiness of the small flat to which he had gone home after work. In the summer, the windows had been thrown open and he had listened to the sound of traffic in the street below as he sat and drank. In the winter, the windows stayed closed, and he drew the curtains early to keep in the warmth.

She used to come up and cook for him. And sometimes, afterwards, they would go to bed. As his drinking got heavier, he had started to miss work, sporadically at first, but then more regularly. They had warned him. And then they fired him. Afterwards, he sat inside and drank more heavily. Until, one day, his money was gone. But, by then, she had left him.

"Why did you leave me?" He asked again.

"Because I couldn't satisfy you. Because I couldn't reach inside and cuddle you. You were always there, beyond me, beyond help. It was useless. We could never have been together."

"You made me feel better."

"But only for a moment. And anyway", she frowned, "I was never sure who you were."

"I was me", Jonah whispered. "I was me."

"And who is me?" she asked. "I felt you, slept with you, and still couldn't break through. You were like a shell, which I held to my ear to listen to the sound of the sea. But there was nothing inside. It was my own senses that made you alive."

Jonah curled up tightly, aware only of the coolness and the brittle bones that housed the void in which he existed. Ahead was the winter, cold and sparse, until the next brief summer and the autumn that followed.

"Do you know who you are?" She prompted him.

"No, because of this memory that is inside me. I don't believe in any afterlife and yet the memories crowd in. Fields I never knew, and people, important people, whose names I can't hear. It's as if they came from a previous life."

"But you don't believe. It's impossible." She stopped. "It's like a graveyard with yew hedges that frightens you at midday. You're afraid of what you will see in the next lane between the hedges. But you know there can't be anything there."

"We ran," Jonah muttered, "both of us."

"There was nothing there." She sounded betrayed.

"Not that day", he said defensively.

"And if we had gone back every day, would there have been something? Would there ever have been anything?"

"Probably not." He felt tired. "The time has passed."

"So, how are you now?" She bent over him, as he lay there, curled on the bank.

"Alone."

"It was always that way", and she ran her fingers through his hair.

"No, at one time I did belong. There were old aunts and uncles and long summer days. I can't remember when the loneliness began. There was a time when it wasn't there."

"But is it true?" She stood up and stared down at him.

"Why would I feel it so strongly?"

"I don't understand how you became as you are." She seemed concerned. "How did you become alone and no longer part of what went before?"

140

"What went before it is gone. It can't be recovered. Even the memory is fading."

He tried desperately to stay awake.

"And what will happen now?" She shook him. "What will happen?"

"Let me sleep. It will just carry on until, one-day, it's over. One day, under a tree, on a cold bench, or on a bloody soiled hostel mattress, it will be over and forgotten. Nobody will remember."

"I will remember."

Her voice was seductive, but he knew she was only a dream. She would forget. She'd already forgotten. And, ahead, there was only the winter to endure.

It was dusk when he awoke. He felt better, refreshed by the sleep, and it was a long walk back into town. He put his coat on and belted it tight around his waist with the coarse string he always used. Grasping his precious red vinyl bag, he set off along the bank. They served soup in the evenings at the hostel. Hot soup that warmed your bones. And Jonah was cold. The days would get colder still but being alive was better than nothing.

ALSO FEATURING JONAH

THE RETURN

It's the start of a nightmare when Laura's former boyfriend discovers she has a new relationship. Darren insists that it's him who decides when their relationship is over, despite Laura ending it when he went to prison. He threatens to punish Andy, her new man, unless Laura agrees to a humiliating proposition. When she refuses, Laura and Andy find themselves facing Darren alone, except for a small number of close friends and, ultimately, the Marsh brothers - two men more frightening than Darren himself.

NO SMOKE WITHOUT FIRE

A few months after his wife and daughter die in a car accident, John Morrison is made redundant and commits suicide. His suicide provokes protests and Jack Docherty, the man who made John redundant, is kidnapped and held responsible for John's death. The kidnappers use sensory deprivation to induce the same emptiness in Jack that drove John to suicide. But the reason for John's suicide may not be as simple as it appears – there are other people who may be equally or more responsible for his death.

ABOUT ROBERT COULSDON

As a child, I wanted to be a hero, like the ones on tv or in films. And so, I made up stories. At first, the stories were mental fantasies, waking dreams in the daytime or imagined adventures at night. But, as soon as I'd learned how to spell and print words, I started to write.

I suppose it was a way of experiencing something more exciting than school and, later, more exciting than work. Something to take me away from the mundane, everyday world, but I never seemed to have the time or discipline to finish anything other than short stories, which is when Jonah came into my life.

I started life in South London, a boy playing on the streets, surrounded by a large family who all lived within walking distance of each other. Then I moved away, to the country and played in woods and made camps, exhilarated by the excitement and freedom. Since then, I've lived in many places, in the UK and abroad, some exciting, some not.

Now, I live by the sea in Southern England and, with fewer distractions, I've found more time to write, and more time to spend with Jonah, sharing the streets and the lives of him and the people who inhabit his world.